JACK O' LANTERN
A Jack of All Trades novel

DH Smith

Earlham Books

Published 2015 by Earlham Books

Book design & cover art by Lia at Free Your Words

(*www.FreeYourWords.com*)

ISBN: 978-1-909804-17-3

PART ONE:
THE CAST & SETTING

Chapter 1

Jack put on goggles and leather gloves. The bottom half of the sash window was broken. Obviously where they'd climbed in. And once inside the classroom, they'd broken the door to get out and into the corridor. Then across the corridor where they'd smashed the door of the computer room... A trail spoored in breakings.

He spread masking tape over the large section of glass still remaining in the frame. Then struck it in a couple of places with a hammer. And took the broken pieces out. And then another hit, and another, removing pieces until most of the glass was gone. He bashed around at the bits left, now confined to the edges, breaking them as close to the putty as he could.

He swept the glass into a heap and put it in the metal bin temporarily. Later he'd bag it up with the rest of his debris and take it down to the dump. But the bin would do for the time being. He wondered who this class belonged to. The displays had been taken down, leaving a metre high area of bare cork on two walls, those without windows or the computer-board.

Jack was wearing a grubby T shirt and jeans stained with paint, realising they could do with a wash as he'd put them on first thing. How many of his building jobs could be traced in their archaeology? So, he'd make them dirtier. His boots were new, hard black. The last lot had cracked and leaked while he was making a cement path. That job done, he'd thrown them out and bought a new pair. Look after your hands and feet; the old mantra, you never knew what shards or grit were lying about in the building game.

A car drew into the car park, making it three vehicles apart from his van. A young woman got out of the car, taking with her a laptop and briefcase. Her hair was tied back in a ponytail; she was slim and dark haired, and could have been anything from twenty-five to thirty-five. She was wearing a brown T-shirt and a green skirt that came below her knees. No paint stains. A teacher, he thought. She locked the car and went into the school.

A light breeze blew through the window. A half and half summer's day, cloud and sunshine. The school quite ghostly, out there just a tractor droning far off on the playing fields. Across the car park a copse of trees to the left, and through them Jack could just make out the glint of a lake. What sort of school has a lake? His was 1960s box-ugly, inner city, with bitumen playgrounds and the playing fields the local park.

Did they row on the lake? Coxed fours or whatever they called it. Did the kids wear boaters and striped jackets?

However did he end up here? Better keep to himself his views on such privilege. They were paying him, and wouldn't feel flattered by the views of a kid from a bog standard comp.

Be a good place for a telescope. All this space. Not that he'd be here when it was dark, past nine o'clock these evenings. But he was always on the lookout where he might take his scope. Areas away from lights and with a wide vista. Out there, maybe on the playing fields, perhaps by the lake. There might be an island in it. Mia, his daughter, would love that. Rowing out as the twilight leaked away to leave dark skies.

He had chipped out the last bit of putty when she came in. The woman who'd got out of the car. She put her laptop and briefcase on the desk by the door. Jack was unsure what to make of her expression. Haughtiness or unhappiness? Either, a builder has to cope with. Understandable, you are trespassing in their space. A pity, though, if his work was to begin with a list of don'ts.

'Hello,' he said cautiously.

'Hello.' She gave him a half smile. It seemed as much as she could manage.

She came over. 'So that's where they got in?'

'I'm putting toughened glass in,' said Jack. 'But...' he added hesitantly, 'to really be effective, all these windows need it.' He indicated the two other sash windows.

'Tell me about it,' she said, throwing up her hands. 'And that's just this classroom. This is a lovely old building but... it eats money.'

She had a very BBC accent, straight out of a costume drama. It almost made him laugh, as if she were putting on a posh accent for his benefit. But that was no way to get on with people, taking the mickey out of their accent. What did she think of his, for that matter? Keep it chatty. So far, she'd been pleasant enough. And not unattractive.

'What happened with the burglar alarm?' he said.

'Well you may ask,' she said. 'It wasn't on. My father... He's the Head.'

'Mr DeNeuve.'

'Ah, you've met him.'

'I wouldn't say I've met him,' said Jack. 'I've been ignored by him.'

'Yes, that's my father. It's beneath his dignity to talk to tradespeople... If you don't mind the description.'

'I've been called worse.'

'I'm Ellie, short for Eleanor, but only my parents ever call me that. Be warned,' she said with a challenging smile.

Which she mitigated by holding out her hand. He shook it, wondering if she did so to spite her father or whether it was genuine.

'I'm Jack Bell.'

'Jack of All Trades,' she said with a laugh.

She'd obviously seen his van. He waited for the comment. Best get it out of the way. Not many he hadn't heard.

'And master of none,' she said. The predictable.

'It's my humility,' he said.

'But not the best of marketing.'

'You won't forget me,' he said.

She looked at him fiercely. She was most definitely sizing him up. Looking for quite what in that quick up and down? Surely not, someone so posh.

'I won't,' she said at last. 'Sorry for the poor joke.'

'Everyone does it,' he said dismissively. 'You were telling me about your father and the burglar alarm...'

She flapped an exasperated hand. 'He often works late here. And forgets to turn the alarm on when he leaves.' She shook her head and sighed. 'Ten thousand quid's worth of computers gone. I doubt the insurance will pay up. And it's not that he has to work here at night. My parents have a house in the grounds, you've probably seen it.'

'The old one, set back as you come in?'

'That's it. I'm sure he comes here just to get away from Mummy. I know he doesn't do much here. Drinks, and I don't know what else.'

'Do you live at the house?'

'Good Lord, no. It's bad enough being here all day, let alone having him all night.'

'Sounds like you don't get on.'

'We have a business relationship.' She stressed business, giving it a cold meaning. 'I don't know why I'm telling you all this.'

'To annoy your old man.'

She laughed. 'You're quite sharp. It does infuriate him that I talk to everyone. I began doing it to put his back up. And then got used to it. But hell, it's the 21st century.'

'With all this...' he gestured around, 'I can't believe many of your friends are, what was the expression? Tradespeople.'

'Hardly any,' she said. 'But I'm not averse. At Oxford one of my friends was the son of a coalminer.'

'But not a coalminer,' he said.

'Well, I did meet him once,' she said. 'A Yorkshire man. Very funny. Witty I mean. I wasn't laughing at him.'

'And what did your posh friends think of him?'

She hesitated for a few seconds, then said, 'They weren't nice. Called the father a chav. And his son too.' She contemplated what she'd just said. 'Stupid really. Territorial. We regard Oxford as ours.'

'And resent the oiks getting in.'

'You wouldn't believe it in this day and age, would you? But the parents of a school like this make great efforts to maintain the class divide...'

'It's in their interest,' he said.

'Precisely.' She laughed. 'Not that I'm a great rebel. It's just I can always see both sides.'

And know where your bread is buttered, he thought, but didn't say.

She glanced up at the wall clock.

'Family meeting,' she said with a sigh. 'Oh dear. I'm not looking forward to this at all. I'd much prefer to stay here and talk to you. But must go.' She went to the desk and picked up her briefcase and laptop. 'Nice meeting you, Jack.'

And she left him to his window.

Chapter 2

Vicky was at her computer, in her small bursar's office, too close to that of her husband, the Head. She would hear him shouting on the phone, all too frequently. If it got bad, she'd put in earplugs which weren't that effective. She'd thought of buying noise-cancelling headphones, but hesitated when she imagined what Graham would say about a woman her age wearing such things. Was his sneering worse than the noise? Though she smiled to herself at the image of him shouting at her while she was wearing them. Stomping and raging while she heard only the Pastoral.

She would get them. Have her own peace. He'd rage whatever she did.

Graham would be in any minute wanting the school budget for the coming year. She'd done it, that wasn't the problem. The important figure was too low. That was the problem.

She was a small, dumpy woman. Too much sitting about in this office fretting and eating cakes. Teachers buy them for too many birthdays, and now she bought them herself for un-birthdays. For the minute or so of relief in cream and jam in the flaky pastry, which only made you yearn for more. She wore no make up, her greying hair tied in a tight bun. She had tried dyeing it, but in the end wondered what for. He didn't care. She didn't care. Sex was dead in their marriage.

She was grey. Let it be so.

Oh, these figures! How to make them dance to his tune. There was really only one source of income, fees from students. They had 124 starting in September, but that wasn't enough. With all the other costs, it left a deficit at the end of the year. Which had to be added to the carried-forward deficits from previous years. It was so depressing. These figures. They gave her a constant headache, they took over her dreams.

It was obvious, they were sinking, but he wouldn't be told.

She took two paracetamol and swallowed them with water. Her head was still fuggy; there'd be some time before they took effect. Work through the fog.

To make the school profitable, she would have to bump the roll up to 157. It wasn't true. There were only three weeks to the beginning of term in September. They might get one or two more pupils, but few parents left it this late to find a school.

She could suggest more cuts, like a Tory Chancellor wielding the hatchet after an election. She'd already looked at further possibilities: lose two teachers, the groundsman, a couple of kitchen staff, and other variations, playing with people like dolls to be discarded from the dolls' house. None of which spelt any hope. Cutting teachers made classes bigger. They could get half a dozen more interns, as she knew they would have to. But they were only youngsters who became resentful at being overused, the teachers resentful at supervising them and undoing their mistakes. Teachers left. It was a downhill spiral.

She was playing with the numbers. A losing game.

The immediate problem was the family meeting. With her two daughters, mummy and daddy, and a budget to present. Oh, she hated this. He'd take one look at the bottom line and say do it again. More students, paper students. Magic them up.

She thought of presenting two budgets. An optimistic one. His one. With 157 students. She'd show him that, hand it out at the meeting, then, when that had been mulled over for a minute or two, deliver the hard-truth budget. Eleanor and Catherine would support her. Not that it would do her much good. Graham would yell, say it was rubbish, ask why she always undermined him – and tear it up. And then back home... She didn't dare to think about back home. The two of them in that big house. Where only the trees could hear you scream.

She had a plan. But it was useless. Because it was her plan and because it transferred ownership. And how often had he told her; DeNeuves have owned the school since before Wellington fought at Waterloo. There were five memorial benches on the side of the hill over the lake, going back to his great-great-grandfather. And portraits of the great and good in the school and even in their own lobby at home.

It was as if, somehow, Graham was claiming Waterloo as a family victory.

She'd told him the bank didn't care whether there was another DeNeuve or not. And what a row that had caused. Belittlement of tradition, magnifying money, undermining family; he'd thrown in the works. She'd shouted back, china was hurled. But he shouted louder than she had, he could go on longer. He had tradition on his side, the drinks cabinet, Waterloo and memorial benches. All she had were numbers.

She'd had it whatever she did. Disaster was rushing their way on a fast horse. They were going bankrupt. Fees would come in at the beginning of term and they could pay off some of their debts, but not enough of them. She would be sent to the bank for another loan. They would say no. Then she'd be sent searching around for another impossible mortgage. It simply took one creditor to stand his ground. When will you pay me, say the bells of Old Bailey. And it would all collapse about their heads, like a house of cards.

She would be blamed, of course. But what happened in a month or two, just possibly stretched to three, didn't matter to him, the meeting in ten minutes did. She'd give him the budget he wanted.

Except her hands wouldn't work. They would not press the keys. She was numbed by thoughts of what was bound to happen. The loss of her house, the school, and the grounds. The house she cared about deeply, well, the school too – but all the penny pinching she had to do, the moans from staff and students about stationery and books. As for the grounds, she never went around them these days. Couldn't enjoy them without seeing money blowing away. Through the trees, scuttling along the fences, sinking in the lake, in a whirlwind across the grass.

But her house she cared about. Mostly the garden at the back where she planted roses, had a herbaceous border and a kitchen garden. Her world away from him and these numbers. She couldn't stand the thought of losing that. Of living with him in a small rented flat somewhere.

She could hear him yelling into the phone. Not the words. They hardly mattered anyway, but the tone, the self righteousness, the bashing of some council official, bank clerk. Someone who differed.

Vicky rose and quickly went out into the hallway. Eleanor was coming towards her. She gave a wave and went the other way.

Chapter 3

Ellie entered the staff room. As usual, she was the first. She looked at the clock. It was going to be one of those meetings. She was on time, the others were late. That always rankled. A ten o'clock meeting should start at ten o'clock. Not twenty past. Waiting made her ratty. Which was never good for the meeting, when first thing on the agenda was her harangue at why no one else could ever get here on time. She'd tried coming late herself but she simply couldn't do it. Couldn't be deliberately late. Felt guilty, had to try so hard to do it. Yet her sister, Cathy, was just naturally late. It was in her make up. Funny really, a mathematician who couldn't calculate time, so was always rushing to catch up with herself. Daddy felt he could be late as he was Daddy, the boss, his privilege. And Mummy always came with Daddy, supporting his lateness.

That left her. In the room, here, on her own. As usual.

It was musty, neglected over the holidays. She flapped her arms about and bashed the cushions against the back of the soft chairs, one by one, throwing up dust. Underused over the summer. It would be busy enough in a few weeks.

When she'd belted every cushion, she went to the window, and lifted it as wide as it would go. And saw the builder, Jack of All Trades, working on the window in her classroom, at right angles to this block. She watched a little while as he hammered round the frame, smiling at the thought of a builder actually admitting his level of competence. Quite cheeky, too, when she was virtually his employer. Though whether he'll ever get paid... Let Mummy deal with that. Jack waved with his hammer at her. She waved back. He was good looking. A builder though. Or tradesman as Daddy would say. No degree, no family. Which was rubbish of course. He meant no estate, no family money. Well, she wasn't planning to marry him. And it would make a change from Clive and his advertising cronies. Making up jingles for chocolate bars.

They'd got bored with each other. With sex, with talking, with bumping into each other in the two-roomed flat. And then she'd become increasingly resentful at the dirty towels and sheets which she always had to wash as if she were his mother, and at the cooking she was expected to do for someone she no longer liked. They'd agreed to split up but were still living together as they had to sell the flat they'd bought jointly, and neither wanted to give it to the other, even temporarily. Both resented the debris and noise of the other, but held their ground. At one point she had considered moving back in with her parents.

And quickly rejected it.

Their house was certainly big enough but she knew she'd revert to a sulky ten year old. Daddy's blasts, her mother's depression. At least with Clive they were on equal terms. Both agreed no sex with anyone else in the flat. Try to be a little civilised. She didn't actively dislike him, just wanted him out of her space. She knew, when it came down to it, she wanted to live on her own.

Not have to wait on and wash for other people.

Ellie put the kettle on and set out four cups. She looked again at the clock. Ten past. What on earth was going on? Well, she wasn't going to go out searching for them. Shouting through the corridors, dragging them in. Not that she'd wanted to be here anyway, except Daddy had called this emergency meeting.

At first she said she wasn't coming. On principle. It was her summer holiday after a too long school year. She changed her mind when he told her Cathy would be here. She would not leave the ground to Cathy.

Though she must not quarrel with her. Above all. Step back, count to ten when she felt it welling. Don't become sisters screaming at who is wearing whose pyjamas. Except this time it would be whose school. Because that, of course, was why they both would be here. The two of them teaching at Bramley, the school they'd gone to as girls. The family estate. The grounds, the lake, the house, the building.

Cathy was not to be trusted.

She dreaded these family meetings. Staff meetings were OK. The family was diluted. And with other staff watching, it was all good mannerly. But the family meetings... Lord God save us! Mummy, Daddy, herself and Cathy in one room together for two hours. There will be yelling, there will be tears.

What bombshell was Daddy about to drop?

Cathy entered, standing at the door for a few seconds, looking about her.

'Just the two of us.' She smiled challengingly. 'How cosy.'

She was the same height as Ellie, hair colouring similar, though without a ponytail. Hers was straight, draped primly down the sides of her face to her chin. They were twins, easy to see in the face and eyes. But not in clothing. Ellie was informal in her wear, Cathy's a navy blue dress suit and a white shirt as if she were about to be interviewed. She carried a black leather briefcase.

'It's not worth coming on time,' she said.

Ellie bit her tongue at the implied criticism of her punctuality. It would be too easy to start. And so easy to predict where it would end, before the meeting itself even got going.

Cathy sat down, eased her skirt about her knees. She opened her briefcase and took out a notepaper pad and a silver fountain pen. She placed them before her on the coffee table.

'Just returned from Thailand,' she said. 'Gorgeous. So ethnic, so spiritual.'

'With Mike?'

Cathy looked at her sharply. 'Of course. We loved the temples. The simplicity of life. We adored the markets. How's Clive?'

'Fine.'

'Been anywhere over the summer?'

'Oh, we've been house hunting.' A lie, a total lie. Cathy always made her do this. The competition.

'Where have you been looking?' said Cathy.

'Oh, here and there. Ingatestone, Danbury. We don't want to go north of the Blackwater. Stay within range of the school.'

'Yes, the school,' said Cathy. 'You don't want to be in North Essex. Though Maldon and Wivenhoe are quite nice.'

'And a decent sized garden,' went on Ellie, constructing her dream. 'South facing. Clive wants to grow grapes.'

'Clive would,' said Cathy.

Her sister's remark almost made Ellie defend her ex. She resisted and went on with her dream.

'Somewhere big enough for a family,' she said. And realised even as the words were streaming out that she would need a Clive, or at least someone male to play a part. If she wanted a family. Weren't there already too many kids in the world? Or at least in the school. She went back and forth on this, daily.

'Are you pregnant?' said Cathy.

'No. Are you?'

'Well actually, I am.' With the brightest of smiles.

'Mummy will be pleased.'

She hoped she had given the hint that she, herself, couldn't give a damn. Though not true. It was one up to Cathy, and Cathy knew it. She tried looking more closely at her sister, without disclosing where she was actually looking. And yes, there was just about a bump. A well aimed boot then.

Heavens, she was dreadful.

'So is the English Dept up to scratch for the new year?' said Cathy.

'Well under control,' she lied. 'And mathematics and science?'

'I did all the planning before we went to Thailand. Daddy has OK'd it. And yours?'

'A little tweaking still to do.'

'Don't leave it too late. You might be the first at meetings but when it comes to the curriculum...'

Ellie wanted to pour the kettle of hot water over her sister's head. Instead said, 'Coffee?'

'Black. No sugar.'

'I know.' I have always known, she thought. She was gritting her teeth, clenching her fists.

'It's the only way I can take instant,' said Cathy.

Ellie could have said that for her. Family clichés. Oh dear, she was washed out and the meeting hadn't even begun.

Their father entered.

He wore a pale-blue suit, including the waistcoat buttoned up, with a watch chain suspended from a pocket. Clothing much too warm for the time of year, but it was, his oft repeated comment, the white man's burden. As if he were surrounded by natives in some Kipling tale of the Raj. He had still a full head of curly hair, with hints of its original ginger though whitening fast, and a thick moustache with a little breakfast egg on one side.

'Where's your mother?' he said brusquely.

Both daughters shrugged with variations of 'don't know'.

'It is twenty past,' he said.

Ellie might have told him that to the minute. Her father, twenty minutes late, expected everyone here waiting for him. She almost clapped her mother for her disobedience, which more than trumped her lateness. It was a rarity.

'She knows we are having a meeting this morning. I don't know how many times I've reminded her,' he said with a long, exasperated sigh. He turned to Cathy. 'Phone her.'

Cathy jerked in annoyance. Her phone was clearly visible in her open briefcase beside her. She could hardly object to the simple request. It was of course the tone that piqued.

'I'll do it,' said Ellie searching for hers.

'No, let me.' Cathy picked up her phone, flipped through the contacts and dialled. 'It's ringing.'

The other two waited, they could just hear the buzz.

'It's gone to voice mail,' said Cathy.

Her father strode across and took the phone.

'Victoria! Where the hell are you? You know we have a family meeting. Get here at once. We need the budget.'

He handed the phone back to Cathy who switched off. And put the phone back in her open briefcase.

'We're not waiting forever,' he said. 'We'd better start.'

'Yes, let's,' said Ellie. 'We are, after all, only 25 minutes late on a day out of our summer holidays.'

'Quite,' said the Head, walking aimlessly about the room. 'I wouldn't have brought you here if it wasn't important, Eleanor.' He stopped in his pacing to gather their attention, which he had 100% anyway. 'We have a situation,' he began again. 'Yes, a situation you might say...' He was working hard to express himself carefully. To not spread alarm. And was of course spreading alarm. 'How we got here is immaterial, but here we are, in time and space. And it's this here and now we have to deal with.'

'Spill, please,' said Ellie barely hiding her frustration.

'Out with it, Daddy,' enjoined her sister.

'A situation...' he said, shaking his Waverley pen which would never be opened. It was the equivalent of a sceptre. '... combining the financial with human resources.' He turned and looked at them both. 'Sandra has resigned.'

This took a few seconds to filter in, as he put the pen back in his top jacket pocket.

'She can't,' exclaimed Cathy. 'She has to give a term's notice.'

He smiled weakly, dropping to the arm of an armchair after his parade.

'She walked out,' he said. 'We had words.'

'I know your words,' said Ellie.

'We both said more than was politic. And the upshot is our deputy head has resigned. Forthwith.'

'She'll get a bad reference,' said Cathy.

The Head shrugged.

'It's illegal,' said Ellie. And turned to the others. 'Isn't it?'

'She's broken her contract,' said Cathy. 'But that hardly helps us.'

'What on earth did you say to her?' said Ellie.

Her father sighed and opened his empty hands, as if it wasn't his fault. 'I told her that we needed more students, that we needed better results...'

Ellie could imagine the conversation. It would consist of blame, one-sided blame. Her father had no finesse. In the family they could talk back to him. Well, she and Cathy could. Mummy had more or less collapsed. But any other underling he bulldozed. Or they left.

'So, we have a vacancy for deputy head,' he said.

'What are we going to do about that?' said Ellie. 'Term starts in three weeks.'

'I thought I'd appoint you as temporary deputy.'

That knocked her back. No way. Not with her father in and out of her office. Get me this, get me that. Phone the

Pope and the Archbishop of Canterbury. It would be hell. Calling her up any time of day or night. No way. In the classroom she was in her own domain. In control. Free, as much as one can be free in a classroom. At least there was no one standing over her barking.

'Why Ellie?' snapped Cathy.

'It had to be one of you,' said the Head reasonably.

'Why Ellie?' snapped Cathy.

'It'll be good for her,' said their father. 'Stretch her.'

'She was always your favourite. Half an hour bloody older and she gets everything in spades.'

Suddenly Ellie realised she did want to be deputy head. More than anything.

'I got a First,' said Ellie quietly.

'You always have a go at me for that two-one. But everyone knows maths is a lot tougher than English. English is barely a subject. It's merely reading. You can do that in your spare time. On a cruise.'

'Your prejudice again, Cathy. Out it comes, term after term. It is obvious to any reasonable person that English is by far and away the most useful school subject. Without it you cannot study any other subject. Even autistic mathematicians have to speak sometimes. And in the real world, we don't go around spouting algebra. Adding up is all you need.'

'And *she* is to be my deputy head?'

'I think so,' said their father.

Cathy rose, her hands flapped to her head. 'This is a madhouse. I have worked my fingers to the bone in this place. The hours I have put in. Marking, talking to parents, after school clubs. And this is the thanks I get.'

'There can only be one deputy head,' said Ellie reasonably.

'Make it joint, Daddy,' demanded Cathy.

'Don't be stupid,' snapped Ellie. 'Can you imagine the two of us working together?'

'Can you imagine me working under you?' She shook her head wildly. 'It's primogeniture gone crazy. Half an hour older and she's the princess. And I'm the slavey. Destiny! I cannot endure this. Will not endure this.' She closed her briefcase with a sharp slap. 'Look at her! A ponytail, like a teenager from Sweet Valley High.' She raised her hands in final surrender. 'This lunatic is leaving Bedlam right now.'

And she strode out of the room, her shoes clacking rapidly down the hallway.

The Head went to the door, half in half out. 'Catherine, come back here!' he yelled. 'Do you hear me? Come back here this instant! We're having a bloody meeting!'

And he was out the door and running down the corridor.

Chapter 4

Some meeting.

She was pleased, though, she'd kept her temper. Pleased Cathy hadn't. She smiled to herself. First one to yell, loses. Admittedly, she was useless at maths, prided herself on it because Cathy was so good at it. Though only a two-one... Some boyfriend-cum-drugs evening the night before the exam, she'd gleaned. And what a twerp he'd proved to be.

If she ever met him again, she'd buy him a drink.

Cathy was well read though. One summer she'd ploughed through every one of Shakespeare's plays. But it was all too late. A two-one branded on her soul. Their degrees swung at each other like laser swords in the hands of Jedi knights. A First could not lose. As her sister had said, destiny.

Three cups of coffee were on the low table. Hers almost drunk, the others almost full. Where was her mother? Or, she might ask, her father and little sister? Alone, she knew she didn't actually want to be deputy head. It would take her out of the classroom too much, and she enjoyed her classroom. She was doing *Jane Eyre* with the older girls. Much better than the done to death *Pride and Prejudice*.

But she had accepted the post, in front of two bloody witnesses. This needed thinking out. How to climb down without losing face? Besides, if she said no, then he'd offer it to Cathy. And Cathy would be her boss.

That was impossible. Had she stuffed herself?

Oh for the simple life! Why couldn't she just go off and shag that builder, without all this family pox? Because of the school. Father had already had a heart attack. Been warned to take it easy, but didn't know the meaning of the word. He

19

would die in harness one day, not too far in the future. And if she was deputy head, then a Black Prince to his King, a dauphin in waiting.

Were there any female equivalents? Some Victoria or Princess Elizabeth...

Her father returned.

'Half a quorum,' she said.

He slumped into the armchair, breathing heavily.

'Would you do me a coffee, dear?'

She handed him one of the cooling cups from the table. He looked at the skin forming on top and put it back on the table.

'Did you catch Cathy?'

'Yes,' he said, patting his beating chest. 'We had words in the car park. Before she drove off.'

'What did she say?'

'That she cannot continue working here if you are deputy head. I said I would be her line manager, not you. But no...' He sighed heavily. 'She said she cannot be so publicly slighted.'

'Only one of us can be deputy.'

'Or none of you.'

Ellie bit a knuckle. Her father was waiting for her reaction, but she said nothing, thinking it out.

He went on, 'She said no deputy head at all. Keep the position vacant while we advertise.'

'And you said?'

'I said, I'd speak with you.' He leaned forward, spreading his hands pleadingly. 'I cannot afford to lose the head of maths and science, Ellie. She is good, I cannot deny it. Knows her stuff, teaches well, is respected. And with three weeks to go... Eleanor, darling. Will you please refuse my offer?'

Ellie was delighted. She had won. She had been offered a position she didn't want. But had felt forced to take it. And now she could be magnanimous, turn it down for the good of her sister. And the school. Of course, she must make it sound a hardship. A position she'd been dreaming of all her life. Squeeze out the gratitude from her father. But she had won hands down, she was the preferred candidate. Still the Black Prince, in all but name.

All she had to do was make sure there was no deputy head.

Chapter 5

Jack tapped in a last glazing sprig with his smallest hammer. And stood back. The glass would hold now until he had the beading ready. It was seated in putty in the frame with four sprigs each side holding it in place. He pressed against the pane with his palms. It was firm. Now to saw the beading to size. Then take out the sprigs one side at a time, with the beading going down to replace them.

He looked at his watch. Twenty minutes more work. The caretaker had invited him over to his house for a tea break. Seemed a nice bloke, friend of Bob's. Jack had brought a thermos, but fresh tea and a chat was always welcome.

His phone rang, the second time in ten minutes. The first he couldn't answer, as he had the glass in the frame but only half the sprigs in and needed a hand on the glass. So out of necessity, he'd let it ring. He didn't like ignoring phone calls. Could be a customer. This job was only a few days' work.

He picked up his phone. Alison. What the heck did she want?

'Hello, Jack,' she said. 'Is this a convenient time?'

'It is now. Was it you phoned ten minutes ago?'

'Yes, it was.'

'Well, I was holding a sheet of glass. I wasn't deliberately ignoring you. OK?'

He was always careful with her. Tempers were fragile with his ex.

'Point taken,' she said curtly. 'I need you to look after Mia the next few days.'

'What?' The woman drove him nuts with her sudden demands. 'I'm working. You're a teacher. On holiday. Why can't you have her?'

22

'I've got to go into hospital tomorrow,' she said. 'A minor operation. Woman's trouble. Sorry to spring it on you. But...'

What could he say to that? He had Mia, their 11 year old daughter, for alternate weekends. That was the drill.

'I understand,' he said, thinking of all the complications, work, food, money, if he had Mia.

'So can you pick her up this evening?'

That shook him. She wanted him to drive down to Brighton, pick up their daughter, and then drive back home again. And look after her for the next few days. He'd got it all now. The total package.

'I'm working full time,' he said. 'Can't you get someone else to look after her? Down there?'

'No, I can't. And I'm going into hospital for an operation. She's your daughter too, you know.'

'I do know,' he said.

Both being stupid, as if she thought he'd forgotten, as if he needed to remind her he hadn't. But he'd known something like this would happen when Alison moved down to Brighton. She was there, he was in London. Some crisis, some time. Alison simply hadn't thought it out when she moved, so eager to take on the new job. And now of all times, when he was so short of cash. He'd have to tell her. Lay it on the table. Life as it is lived for a builder.

'I haven't got any money,' he said. 'I can't come to Brighton.'

'What?' she exclaimed. 'None at all?'

'Penniless.'

It was true. All he had were a few coins. Apart from that, he was spent to the bottom of his overdraft.

'What about all that money you had?'

'Who told you about that?'

'Who'd you think? Mia, of course.'

Little pitchers.

'So have you spent the lot?' she went on, obviously appalled by his spendthrift ways. 'All of it?'

'I bought my flat,' he said.

'And didn't leave yourself a cushion?'

'I needed most of it for the down payment,' he said. 'I've got to live somewhere. Anyway, I'm working, should get paid soon, but at the moment I'm clean out of cash.'

'Can you get to London Bridge station at 6 pm?'

'Yes, but...'

'Be there. I'll bring her up by train. I'll sub you twenty quid. Don't drink it.'

He bit his tongue. The cow. He had to take her charity along with her barbs.

'Some of us don't happen to get paid regularly,' he said as reasonably as he could. 'We're not all teachers. It's up and down in the building game. I'm not sitting home on my arse if that's what you think. I'm earning. It's just that...' he floundered a second then added, 'It's what they call cash flow.'

'London Bridge at six. Don't be late.'

She rang off.

He could easily have put his fist through the window. So easy for her as deputy head of a primary school. Regular money coming in every month. She simply wouldn't understand what it was like for someone on an uncertain, self-employed income. Or maybe it was because it was him. Dwelling on how their relationship ended. But he'd noted too frequently how those with safe jobs, regular monthly incomes, thought the rest of the world were skivers, watching daytime TV and getting drunk.

A sympathy deficit. Well, screw her.

It was a struggle, just keeping his head above water. He'd stayed sober for well over a year now. Went twice a week to Alcohol Halt. But this was a lousy time for a small builder. Too many short jobs, then nothing while he put feelers out and counted his pennies. Bob had got him this one. OK, he'd had some luck last year and got some unexpected money. But then his flat came up. It was either buy it or move out. The landlord wanted a quick sale. He had enough cash for the down payment, and with some exaggeration of his income, lies to be exact, managed to get a mortgage. And now he struggled to pay, month by month.

He'd love a cushion. A builder always needs some cash in hand for materials, petrol, tools. It was no good this begging Peter to pay Paul. But what could he do about it?

Sod her. He cringed at having to tell her he didn't have the money to get down to Brighton. But there you are. All said. All arranged.

How she charged him up.

Calm down. Get some of the beading in. Then tea break with the caretaker. And don't forget London Bridge station at 6 pm. Work. And leave the worry of how to manage Mia and this job for later.

It was then it came to him. He could've got a payday loan. Needn't have said a word about him being broke. Could phone Alison back on that. But no, he didn't want to speak to her again. And payday loans were poison. Astronomical interest.

He got out his tenon saw and mitre box. Work. Get into the swing of it. The long beading rod was already marked up. He lay it in the box on a piece of old cardboard, slid the saw into a 45 degree slot, and began gently sawing. Slowly does it. As he got near the end of the cut, he slowed further, letting his fingers take the weight as the end fell away without a snag.

Perfect.

If only the rest of his life could be this way.

Chapter 6

Graham DeNeuve was seated on a memorial bench for his father, watching a pair of coots aimlessly swimming, dipping from time to time in the dark green water, the white on their small heads like hopeless handkerchiefs to keep out the sun.

What goes on in those tiny brains as they swim in circles? he reflected. Much less than even some of his students. Never a Gauguin of the Lake, a Shakespeare of the Reeds. But just enough brain to stay alive and breed.

What is the point of a life like that? Aimless circles.

His father knew the answer. God. He gave the coots life and gave man dominion over them. A belief he, himself, held when he was a choirboy, when his father was Head. But without God there was simply a coot, nonsensically pretty in its black feathers and white skull cap, swimming like a toy, driven by the batteries of hunger and sex.

He had learnt to row on this lake. His father gave him his first lessons. Probably brought God into it somewhere; it was so long ago he couldn't remember. But his father brought God into most things. And he'd learnt the Platonic trick himself; the design of the boat, the oars, were God-given. He'd said such things in school assemblies. Thank God for this and that. For coots and sunsets, for computers and friendship. He was up there, in Heaven, directing the world. Watching every little coot, on every little lake.

It was his daughters' questions that first made him doubt. When they were small. Although he gave them the gospel his father had given him, he would then go away and think about the holes in his pat answer. Pull apart the snags, until he was left with disconnected threads. Broken shoelaces.

His father knew. He would say it was God's plan for him to be the Head after him. Was never cursed by why. The devil's interrogative. It was God's plan, the whole answer. If Graham could ask him why the school was going broke, supposing there was some bit of his father floating somewhere in the cosmos who could respond, his father might have referred him to the Book of Job.

Suffering, like the coot, had a purpose.

If there was a God.

And if there wasn't?

There was simply suffering. Bills were bills, not trials set by God. Not steps on Jacob's ladder with Heaven on the top rung, but the hard change of things without the small print of eternal life.

Real life.

At least he'd persuaded Eleanor not to take on the deputy headship. Thank goodness for that. He could have rescinded the offer, of course. But then he'd have two rowing daughters. Much better that she had seen why she could not have it. For now anyway.

By which time, Catherine had gone off in a huff. He'd left her several messages on voicemail, several texts. If there was no God, there must be family.

The only hope in all this.

God knew where Victoria was. Or did He? Presumably yes. No bird falls from a nest without Him knowing. And when the fox eats it for breakfast...

Why had she abandoned him?

The meeting had accomplished what? That there was to be no deputy head, but that really was the minor item. Money, next on the agenda, was the big one. But with Catherine doing a runner and Victoria not there to present the budget, he could not give them his plan.

A swan had come out from round the island. He watched its stateliness, the beauty that princesses had in fairy tales, as it progressed over the water, ripples trailing in its wake and sparkling in the sunlight. He could imagine it was there just for him. To soothe him, to placate him. To put his little world in perspective.

And remind him of the world to come.

How would that go down with the bank manager? If he showed him pictures of swans and coots, instead of cash flow and the balance sheet.

Graham withdrew a bottle of Evian water from his pocket. Miraculously, it had been turned into gin.

Chapter 7

When she stopped at the lights Cathy glanced at the incoming texts. Ellie was not taking up the post of deputy head. Would she please come back and continue the meeting?

She laughed. Her father was always too late with his diplomacy. There was voicemail too. Doubtless from him. Probably saying the same thing. Praise and pleading, after the fact.

Well, she would not answer her phone for a while. Leave them uncertain. Though he had managed to catch her at the school car park, which perhaps was a pity, or perhaps not. She'd laid out her demands and then driven off.

And it worked.

Now let them sweat.

A hoot from behind revived her. The lights had changed. Cathy put her foot down and eased away from the traffic lights. She was certainly not going to do an about turn. If her father was going to be so stupid, then let him and Ellie waste a day. Next time he might think first.

As for Ellie, she might even wish the job on her. That would be a delightful ruse. Tell her sister that she'd thought about it and Ellie was welcome to the job. Let father kick her around for a few weeks, see how much she wanted it then. For Cathy was under no illusion. It was not a desirable post. Poor Sandra had been having a terrible time. Amazing she had stood it for two years.

She'd phone her tonight. Tell her she'd work on father, so she didn't get a bad reference. Even Ellie would agree to that. For Sandra had been her and Ellie's umpire often enough in their various staff room wrangles.

Good luck to Sandra. She was better off out of it. Bramley was a family trial.

The traffic was light on the country road, mid morning. The sun shining, and she was out of school. Like a sixth former playing truant. Such a relief to be driving. To be in control, in her car, going her way. And having them wait on her.

She wondered who had won. Her walking out was a point for Ellie. And Ellie magnanimously climbing down. A second point. But then Cathy had made her. And was making them wait on her decision. So was it a draw? Father would not dare do it again. She was the senior maths teacher. She could get a job anywhere. English teachers were two a penny. She had been head hunted by a public school, she'd informed him in the car park, and it wasn't too late to turn the offer down.

Pure bluff. Not the head hunting. But she wasn't taking it up. She wasn't leaving Bramley to Ellie. Maybe she shouldn't have walked out, she conceded, but then it wasn't working out so badly. The school needed her. Better if she'd laid it on the line then and there. Been in the room when her father had to rescind his offer. Instead of a teenage tantrum.

Why does one revert? Suddenly, you are thirteen again, powerless... Next she'd be cutting her arms or starving herself. How does one grow up? Be an adult in the family. Or at least pretend to be. Maybe that was the best you could do. Act. Until you'd convinced yourself. After all, she had the trump card. The school needed her. It could cope without a deputy. It could manage without a head of English. Others could fill in, temporary staff. But maths teachers were gold.

Any new graduate could work a page ahead in *Pride and Prejudice*. But teach Binomial Theorem and Newton's Laws of Motion? Oh, she must stand her ground. Remind them how much they needed her. Make her demands.

She pulled in to the roadside café. She brushed her hair in the mirror and renewed her lipstick. Smart, well-dressed, attractive – who would know of her tantrum? If only you could wipe away such things, instead of carrying the bruise. A bruise on a bruise. Peel off the crust, how far down could you go before you found virgin cells? She had a friend who had done ten years of psychoanalysis and to Cathy's eyes seemed no better. Though her friend said she would be even worse without it.

She took her briefcase and got out of the car. She smoothed herself down and locked up. For an instant she stayed on the spot. A good car, a well tailored suit. Walk like it was meant to be.

Everything was an act.

Her mother, seated at the window, waved to her.

Chapter 8

Jack came to the gatehouse, and felt quite envious. It was a two storey, red brick house with high chimneys. There was a low, trimmed box hedge in front, and dahlias and chrysanthemums lining the crazy-paving path to the open front door. He walked down the path and looked in the open doorway. The hall was full of tea chests, cardboard boxes and plastic bags tumbling out with clothing, bedding and miscellanea.

He called, 'Hello? It's Jack. The builder.'

The caretaker came out of a back room to greet him, edging his way between the boxes. He was a middle aged man, muscular with a suggestion of spread about the middle. His face was weathered, and he had short receding hair, dyed too brown.

'Excuse the mess, Jack.'

Jack had met him earlier when he'd first come. They had a mutual friend in Bob. The caretaker had shown him the work to be done. And invited him over later for tea break.

'I wouldn't have come, if I'd have known you were so busy, George.'

The caretaker held his hands up. 'It's OK, mate. It means we can stop this packing lark for fifteen minutes. Come out back. It's civilised there.'

He led Jack along the hallway, through the kitchen which was just about a kitchen with the essentials still there. But Jack noted a sitting room in passing which was stripped, shelves empty, and bare light bulbs. They went out the kitchen door to the garden. On the patio was a round iron-work table with four chairs to match. On the table were tea things, with a pile of toast and jam and a plate of buns.

Seated at the table was a very harassed woman, hair straggly and a dust streaked face.

'Please sit down, Jack,' she said. 'Bob told us all about you.'

He sat down, wondering what Bob had said, presumably favourable seeing the spread. He couldn't avoid the obvious.

'You're moving.'

The caretaker laughed, but with little merriment. 'You noticed?'

She frowned. 'Oh what a pain! You would not believe what we've accumulated in seventeen years... I'll pour the tea.'

She poured three mugs. Jack added milk to his, hungry enough for this unexpected feast.

'Bob said treat you well,' she said.

'He's a good mate, Bob,' he said. 'Stood by me when things were rough.'

'He's helping us move,' said the caretaker. 'Driving the lorry on Saturday.'

'Got somewhere to go?' A silly question, he instantly thought, or why drive a lorry.

'Some hole in the wall place,' she said angrily. 'Thank God the boys are at my mother's.'

'New job?' said Jack.

The caretaker shook his head. For a second he didn't speak, buttering the bun on his plate with some deliberation.

'One month's notice,' he said. 'Seventeen years and we got one month's notice.'

'I hate those DeNeuves,' she said fiercely.

The caretaker held a hand up. 'Jenny!'

'I don't care who knows it. And he's a friend of Bob's anyway. Mr DeNeuve,' she poked out a tongue, 'Mr do this, do that. Now!' She growled, her hands clawing the air. 'I'm catering manager, as was. Miss Catherine DeNeuve. Miss

Hoity Toity, nose in the air, can we have Colombian coffee? As if I didn't know her when she was a spotty twelve year old...'

'Ellie is alright,' said George.

She sniffed. 'To you maybe. Though why Head of English should have anything to do with catering...' She stopped herself. 'Oh, what's the point going on? We're out of here. That's the one good thing. We are leaving Bramley forever.'

'Both of you have lost your jobs,' said Jack, somewhat exhausted by the thought. 'And the house too?'

'Oh, I shall miss this place,' she said, her arms indicating the house and garden. 'All my vegetables. My autumn planning about to begin, each garden year with the catalogues, sowing the seeds... It was totally run down when we moved in, and year by year I've added to it. Made it.'

Behind her Jack could see beanpoles, cabbages, tomatoes – a full summer's growth of leaf and fruit.

'He was half pissed,' said George. 'Came up and gave me an envelope. I didn't know what it was, so I left it a while. Then when I read it, I couldn't be sure what I was reading... I ran up here.'

'One month's notice,' she said. 'On the house and on both our jobs. Seventeen years all over in one fell swoop. Damn the DeNeuves.'

'Clear your things and get out,' he said. 'All settled here, with a family. It's an earthquake.'

'Such a beautiful house,' said Jenny. 'Roomy. Great for the kids. No travel. Garden. I've got a workroom for my sewing and knitting.'

'Not quite heaven,' said George. 'Always on beck and call. Evenings, weekends, specially with the DeNeuves just a hundred yards away... But could I get a better place than this?' His hand swept about the garden and house.

'I always knew it would come,' exclaimed Jenny. She put her hands to her face and closed her eyes. Then remembered her duties. 'More tea, Jack?'

'Thank you, Jenny.'

She poured. 'Tied house. Great when you get it. Couldn't believe it when we first saw it. Lovely place in all these grounds. We decorated every room, painted. Created the garden. Then when I had the boys, still plenty of room.' She stopped. 'But it was never ours. They always had it over us. Lose the job, then you lose the house... It's been my nightmare.'

'But they'll still need a caretaker and catering manager,' said Jack. 'Surely?'

'Oh, some company is taking it all on,' said George through gritted teeth. 'Shag 'em and Wag 'em something or other Services. I don't know what it's bloody well called. They bring in some underpaid flunkies...'

'Then see how the ugly sisters are going to moan,' added Jenny.

'There's a dodgy boiler,' said George with a smirk, 'in the basement, supplying all the hot water and radiators. Took me months to learn how to handle it. They won't know. Probably have a different guy in each week.'

'They'll be phoning you up,' said Jenny.

'I'll tell them where they can stuff it,' retorted George.

'No you won't,' she said. 'You'll need a reference.' She put down her mug. 'They still have a hold on us. I want to strangle them. But it's still yes, Mr DeNeuve, thank you very much Mrs DeNeuve. Please kick us some more.'

'Just wait,' said George. 'Wait till that boiler packs in. And see what parent'll pay fifteen thousand a year for a cold school...'

'And lousy food,' added Jenny. 'They are that fussy. Them DeNeuves.'

'Fifteen thousand!' exclaimed Jack. 'What am I doing here?'

'It's clear enough why,' said George. 'Not that I blame you.'

'What d'you mean?'

'One man band, that's you, right?'

'Well, I work on my own. Mostly.'

'You're cheap, Jack. I don't mean to demean your work. But cheap is the name of the game round here.'

Chapter 9

Cathy looked at herself in the mirror of the café and frowned. The same face she always saw. The one she was stuck with. Ellie's too, the constant reminder of the split ovum. Neither had taken the cuckoo's chance and removed the other.

She had slipped off her shoes under the table. When she was at school, she changed into flats, ditto when she was driving. Quite stupid really, these shoes. As if she was always on stage, always in the spotlight. She had too many costumes, too many shoes. A frequent, unremarkable neurosis.

She must stop looking at herself in the mirror.

They were on their second coffee and cake. She'd read her texts, they were still coming. And had listened to her voicemail. Vicky had picked up hers too. Neither of them were replying.

'He's had his chance,' said Vicky.

'He's had a hundred chances,' said Cathy.

'If we leave it to him, we lose it – and that's that. Bramley gone, tradition or no tradition.'

'Your figures are clear enough.'

Cathy had a copy of the budget in front of her. The story was easy enough to read with a little competence in these things. And Cathy easily had that.

Vicky wiped the cream off her top lip with a finger. And licked it clean.

'The only show in town is Lady Margaret's,' she said.

'Are you sure we can trust her?'

Vicky shrugged. 'Pretty sure. Can I say one hundred per cent? No. But she's an old girl, wants Bramley to continue. And she's offering a generous leaseback.'

'It will never wash with Daddy. We won't own Bramley. That's all he'll be able to see.'

'We'll still be living there, in the house, in the grounds. And Lady Margaret says we can buy it back gradually with future profits.'

'If there are any profits.'

'There has to be,' said Vicky. 'Your father must step down.'

'He won't.'

'The three of us must confront him.'

'Three of us?'

'Eleanor has to be part of this. We must be of one mind.'

Cathy shuddered and shook her hands. 'Me and Ellie agreeing? Working together?' She gave a half laugh. 'When the Sun explodes.'

'It has to be. If we want Bramley in any shape or form.'

'Suppose then, just suppose we depose Daddy... Who becomes Head?'

Vicky looked her daughter in the eye and gave a tight-lipped smile. Her daughter's thoughts and fears were too obvious. She could feel the hell of the years to come, but there was only one way.

'Me,' she said. 'I will be Head.'

Cathy was caught open mouthed, half chewed cake on her tongue. Realising, she covered her lips and swallowed.

'You have no teaching qualifications, Mummy,' she blustered.

'I don't need them,' she said. 'Bramley is a business. It needs to be run as a business.'

Both were silent, drinking coffee, watching the comings and goings in the car park. Plotting the revolution and imagining the aftermath.

'I have been to hundreds of staff meetings,' said Vicky. 'I know the drill. I won't be doing any teaching. There'll be a gang of three to run the place. As a business.'

'He won't agree. And Bramley is his.'

'Then we'll have to take another course. But whatever we do, we need Ellie on board.'

'Oh my God,' moaned Cathy. 'Another bloody family meeting.'

'The three of us. And no walkouts.'

Cathy's eyes went to the figures in front of her, as if there might be an algorithm that had been missed. Some x that could be pretending to be a y. But it was too simple. Student numbers. Their heaven and their hell.

'Where do we meet?' she said.

'The house.'

'Suppose he comes back?'

Vicky shook her head. 'He never comes back these days. Stays in the school all day. Likes to look busy even when he's doing nothing. The portraits looking down on him, his closed office door… He can pretend he's a Head.' She looked at her watch. 'Say two o'clock. I'll phone Eleanor.'

'Will she come?'

'I'll tell her her future depends on it.'

Chapter 10

Jack had been invited back to the gatehouse for lunch, but the place depressed him. The garden was pleasant but the hardship of the caretaker and his wife was inescapable. And it was all they could talk about. He told them he was just taking a short break for lunch, wanting to get as much done as possible.

That was true enough. He wanted to be away, feeling uncomfortable in this environment. Fifteen thousand a year to swim in the lake, play on the fields with hockey sticks and cricket bats. Out here in Billericay. You'd never think it. Though some of the houses he'd passed coming in... Yes, there was money here. Golf courses and lakes.

He was sitting on the edge of the copse above the lake munching a sandwich. There was an island in the middle of the lake so he could not make out where it ended. To his right were the playing fields. A flat expanse of privilege. All this space. Small classes. How the rich gave their offspring a heave up the ladder. He felt itchy, like a heretic in a church. As if somehow they would know and turn on him as a comprehensive school boy.

There was a breeze breaking up the surface of the lake. Near the boathouse and its landing stage, ducks were swimming, oblivious of costs and ownership. He could imagine a regatta with long, slender rowing boats being carried out of the boathouse, children and parents cheering, bunting flapping. Strawberries and cream.

And cash tills ringing.

Jack wasn't hungry, eating out of duty. The tea break at the gatehouse had gone on rather long, and he'd been offered more buns and toast every time his plate emptied.

But for lunch, it was not so much the eating, he'd wanted a break from the classroom. He felt trapped in the school, diminished, with imagined teachers shouting, telling him he had no right. No right at all. To what, a little vague. Some original sin in being working class.

Not that he'd liked school. Found it crushing. And got out as soon as he could, with damn all in qualifications. This place was a reminder of his failure, with the added chorus of the ruling class saying it would never be different.

It was work. He couldn't afford to be fussy. Do the job and go home to the hoi polloi in Forest Gate. Don't fight the class war. Saw, bang in nails and put in new glass.

He would need to tell the caretaker to paint the window beading in a couple of weeks. Then remembered the caretaker wouldn't be here. And wouldn't give a damn if the window beading was painted or not. He'd leave a note. Tell Ellie.

Then he saw her coming down the hill towards him. Slim, a fine figure. He had the feeling she had been eyeing him up earlier. He'd certainly been looking her over. But she was out of his class... Jenny hated her. Along with the other DeNeuves.

Posh totty, Bob might have said.

Anyway, whatever his hormones compelled, he had Mia to pick up this evening. Love life on hold.

She had a sandwich in one hand, a bottle of water in the other, and a red handbag on a long strap over her shoulder, as she sauntered towards him along the line of trees on the crest of the hill. Her pony tail bounced on her back. As she came in, he saw she was wearing sandals, and her toenails were painted red.

'Do you mind if I join you?' she said with a bright smile.

'I should ask your permission to be here.'

She sat down. 'It's not exactly crowded today.'

She unwrapped her sandwich, brown grainy bread with ham, thick with salad poking out the edges.

'Our family meeting was a waste of time,' she said. 'As usual. But I note you've done better. The window's in.'

'It'll need painting in a couple of weeks. When the putty's set. I'll work on the door this afternoon.'

'Quite a mess they made of it,' she said.

'Burglars don't care,' he said, and took a last bite of cheese sandwich. Save the other one for mid afternoon. He poured some more tea from his thermos into the cup. 'I would offer you...'

She shook her head. 'Water's fine. Purifying.' She took a swig, then wiped her mouth with the back of her wrist. 'I was offered the deputy headship today.'

'Congratulations.'

She laughed. 'My sister went bananas. We're twins, you know. I used to read about twins when I was a kid here. The ones who did everything together. Best friends, bosom buddies. Inseparable.' She reflected. 'I suppose we were inseparable. It's this damn place. Couldn't get away from each other. Teachers always comparing us to each other. Other kids doing the same. And then like a couple of homing pigeons, we both came back to Bramley to teach.'

'Plenty of other schools,' said Jack. 'Why here?'

'Look at it,' she said.

'I have,' he said, though perhaps he was looking at her more.

'Neither of us wanted the other to get it. So if she was here, I had to be. Simple. And quite stupid.' She flapped a hand dismissively and then went on. 'Daddy's health is bad. So one of us is going to take on the mantle fairly soon.' She turned to him and shook her head. 'It's not yet decided who that will be. Today, I had to decline the deputy headship. For family peace.' She bit her lip. 'I think one of us will have to kill the other to settle it.' She smiled at him, as if it was all light hearted banter. 'Your family any better?'

'I haven't seen my parents in two years,' he said. 'I had a drunken phase and got quite out of control. I keep meaning to phone my mother, then I don't.'

'It seems a pity not to,' she said, and then added after a pause, 'but I don't know what you did.'

'Stole fifty quid out of her purse and got drunk for four days.' He didn't know why he was saying this to her, except his mother had been on his mind, and maybe he wanted someone to tell him it wasn't so bad. Or maybe square up to her family dysfunction.

'She didn't call the police?' she said.

'No,' he said looking out across the lake at a heron in a tree. 'But I've felt so guilty... Stealing money from my mother.'

'Not quite Oedipus,' she said.

He tried to think who Oedipus was. He'd heard of him, some sex thing and the Greeks, but couldn't connect it with what he'd been saying. He didn't want to ask her to explain.

'Anyway,' he said, 'it's too nice a day to talk about my drunken exploits. I will phone her.'

'You seem alright now. Or is it Dr Jekyll I'm speaking to?'

'I've been on the wagon for 18 months. When I was a drunk, I behaved like a demented ape. My wife kicked me out. We're divorced now. I've got an eleven year old daughter who lives with her mum...' He hesitated a second, not wanting to queer his pitch, but maybe he had already with his talk of his drunkenness. 'I've got her the next couple of days... Her mum's going in to hospital. What I'm going to do with Mia, I haven't the slightest.'

'Bring her here.' He looked at her to confirm she was serious. 'If she can entertain herself, we've got the library, masses of books, loads of movies, computers... You could take her out to the island for a picnic. I used to love that. Felt like a pirate.'

'You could come too,' he said.

She smiled. 'I might.'

'How do you get over?' he said, indicating the sweep of water.

'Take a boat from the boathouse. Plenty there.'

'Won't your father kick up a fuss?'

She reflected. 'Not if I came with. Though he might afterwards. I shouldn't be fraternising with tradesmen.'

'Not with your expensive education.' And la-di-da voice, he might have added.

'One gets tired of public schoolboys,' she said. She had finished her sandwich and wiped her hands on her jeans. 'I appreciate honest work.' She sighed. 'I hate what we've done to the caretaker and his family.'

'They're not too fond of you lot.'

'And why should they be? We've done the dirty on George and Jenny Grove. But it isn't so simple. This place is in trouble, moneywise. In fact, we could easily go bankrupt. And then we are all out on our ear.'

'Then you'd have to marry a fat merchant banker.'

'Oh heaven save me from that. I know a few. Boredom in pinstripes.' She stood up. 'Do you want to see the boathouse?'

'Yes.' He rose and stood by her side. 'I've not had that invitation before.'

'It's not everyone I'd ask,' she said as they strolled down the hill to the lakeside. 'In fact,' she began conspiratorially, 'it's where we used to go when we were in the fifth form. To smoke. And to kiss the boys.' She laughed at her own memory. 'I haven't been inside for a couple of years. But I still have a key. At least I think I do.' She took out her bunch of keys from her handbag and sorted through them. 'This one, I think. That's if they haven't changed the lock.'

A pair of coots swam eagerly towards them.

'No bread,' she exclaimed, showing them her empty hands.

Jack considered sacrificing the half of sandwich he had left, but decided against it.

'It's a beautiful lake,' he said.

'Just over 250 metres long,' she said. 'Just right for our races. Lots of fierce sprints.'

They arrived at the boathouse.

'Too many wasted afternoons here, puffing away,' she said.

And kissing boys, he thought.

'No. They haven't changed the lock. Should really.' Then reflected. 'Though it's not likely someone would steal a boat.'

She put the key in and turned it. Then pulled open one of the double doors. And almost immediately slammed it shut. But not quickly enough. For Jack had seen exactly what she had seen.

A stack of computers.

She took a step back, then said awkwardly, 'I don't think so. Not today.'

He wondered whether the picnic on the island would be out tomorrow. What with the boathouse full of contraband.

'I saw,' he said.

She waved her hands frantically. 'This is terrible. I don't know who is doing what.' She looked to him nervously. 'You won't say anything?'

'It's nothing to do with me,' he said. 'Some insurance fraud. Why should I give a toss?'

She kissed him.

Chapter 11

Jack was paying little attention to his work. The builder in him had a door to finish, but the animal had other priorities, none of which involved carpentry. He was here to work, he told himself. To earn money. But his coursing hormones had no interest in money. Somehow he continued working, measuring up the section of doorjamb he'd have to remove, went to write it in his notebook, but had forgotten the figure in the two paces.

He tried to convince himself of the simple truth; they were in different universes. Woodcutters do not marry princesses. So – the doorpost. Concentrate. The door itself wasn't salvageable. The caretaker had a couple of spares in the basement, plus a range of timber. So Jack wouldn't have to be out buying. With what anyway? The doorjamb was broken in the middle where the thieves had forced the door. The choice was replace the whole length of the jamb or take out the broken bit and screw in a new piece. He'd gone for the latter. If he did it carefully, it would be just as strong, wouldn't show after painting, and he wouldn't have to replace any beading.

Sex obtruded. It was as if he had two televisions on with separate programmes and was trying to concentrate on the quieter one.

A pity Mia was coming later. And staying for how long, he wasn't sure. He'd find out from Alison at the station. That was the way of things. Complications. Commitments. Ellie was vibrant, beautiful, easy to get on with. Admittedly her family were doing the dirty on the caretaker and his missus. Ellie was sorry, but that was no help to the caretaker.

Such scruples his body had no time for. Go for it.

He was working at half speed. Reflecting all the time on what had happened at the boathouse. The embrace begun at the front, slid round to the back and continued on the bank of the lake, ignored by the coots. Clearly, the grappling couple were not going to give them bread.

They'd been interrupted by a phone call, which Ellie had answered huffily. Jack gathered that it was from her mother, and that Ellie was wanted at the house. Ellie complained she was working. But her mother was insisting, and then her sister had come into it. Ellie became angry, saying she'd already given up the deputy headship for her sake... And then Ellie had walked further away, wanting more privacy, and he'd caught a mention of her father, but little else.

They'd parted with a lingering kiss, she heading to the house, he to the school.

With square and tape, he measured and marked up. The jamb would need careful sawing. All the better. That might keep his mind on the job. In 90 minutes he'd have to leave to meet Alison and Mia, and wanted to get as much done as he could. Long tea breaks and cuddles behind the boathouse didn't earn you money.

A bit of drilling to get him started. To block out the extraneous noise. The hiss and burr of steel into wood, the gripping of the handle and shaft. And then in sawdust and wood shavings, he became a carpenter for an hour.

Chapter 12

Ellie and Cathy sat on the two side armchairs, and Vicky on the sofa between, ready to play the referee.

'So you'd be Head,' said Ellie to her mother. 'And then what?'

'Depends how long I live,' said Vicky. 'In maybe ten years, we could be clear of debts.'

'Fine, as far as it goes,' said Ellie. 'But Daddy won't agree to any of it. You as Head? What's he going to be doing all day? Making dinner, doing the shopping and ironing?'

'Reluctant as I am to agree with my sister,' said Cathy, 'it's all too clear. Bramley is his. Through his family. He won't give it up.'

'It's mine, when he dies,' said Vicky.

'That's not helpful, unless you have plans in that direction,' said Ellie dismissively.

'I do,' said Vicky. 'And that's why I have you both here.'

Ellie looked from one to the other. Cathy showed no surprise; they'd been discussing it already, she thought. The forbidden. They wanted her approval. She couldn't believe it. Surely not?

'There can be only one solution,' said Cathy.

'The two of you have it all worked out,' she exclaimed, looking from one to the other. 'You ran out of the office this morning,' she directed to her mother, and then to her sister, 'and you threw a wobbly at the meeting. All arranged. So you could conspire.'

'Not quite so well organised, Ellie,' said Vicky. 'We took advantage of the fact.'

'Daddy is out of control,' said Cathy. 'Surely even you can see that.'

48

'Thank you for your faith in me,' said Ellie blowing a raspberry. 'And if I have now caught up with you two, and if I am not reading you wrong, it seems the two of you have decided to do him in. And you want me to agree. Is that so?'

'Would you rather Bramley went into receivership?' said Cathy.

'Blunt instrument, gun or poison?' said Ellie. 'Have you decided the means? Or just the ends?'

'Don't be such an obstreperous fool,' exclaimed Cathy. 'We're here, not somewhere else. Bramley is going down the chute hellishly fast. What other solution have you got?'

'Cathy dearest, I object to walking into a room where all the decisions have been made beforehand,' said Ellie with mock politeness. 'What's the point of me being here?'

Cathy threw her hands up. 'I knew it would be this way. Unless she makes the decision, no one else is allowed to.'

'It's you, always wanting to control the agenda. And when you can't – you walk out.'

'Hark at Daddy's favourite charmer! Nearly had your hands on Bramley this morning. One hundred per cent bankrupt stock! That's my sister, all the way. Shagged your builder yet?'

'Why? Do you want him?'

'I saw you at the boathouse. Just like the old days. Have you put your knickers back on?'

'I hope you're recording this, Mummy.'

Vicky sighed. 'Five minutes with the two of you and I am exhausted. Please, put enmity aside and concentrate. Once we've settled Father, then I'll have a document made up – giving you both half of Bramley when I pass away. All yours. So there's none of this squabbling about who gets what. In the meantime, there has to be a Bramley. Or you both get bugger all.'

Ellie knew she must clamp down the fury that meetings with her sister always stoked. She began breathing in and out slowly, counting to herself. One of them said something, the other reacted – and they were off. From time immemorial. That stuff about her knickers. Playground stuff. Mind you, another quarter of an hour at the boathouse and who knows? But how could Cathy be so holy? She could get through a football team. Stop. Think. Breathe.

She crossed her fingers on both hands and held them up.

'Pax,' she said.

Cathy gave a sniffy laugh. This was their childhood truce. Enabling them to talk, change the rules, before they started fighting again.

'Pax,' said Cathy, holding up her own crossed fingers. 'I'll make us all a coffee. And even trust you to talk with Mother while I'm out.'

Chapter 13

The doorjamb was repaired, the piece screwed in neatly. A little filler and paint and you wouldn't know it was there. Should he leave it for today or hang the door? He looked at his watch, he had to get to the station to meet Alison and Mia. Well, he could at least bring the door up and be ready for the morning. And with luck be able to finish this door and the one on the computer room tomorrow.

The door was in the basement, where the caretaker kept assorted items that might be useful one day. Jack went out into the corridor to go downstairs, and there, maybe fifteen metres away, he saw a man lying flat out, face up.

What was this?

He ran over, stood over him and recognised him as the Headmaster. His first thought was heart attack. Jack knelt down, and at that level smelt the alcohol. Drunk. He knew this situation well enough, but from the other side. Jack loosened the man's tie. And wondered what else to do.

In a similar position himself a few years ago, he'd somehow woken up in hospitals, in strange houses, on a park bench once. Now what to do? He shouldn't really leave him here. The Head needed to be taken somewhere where he could be kept an eye on. Jack thought of phoning George, the caretaker. But then George might not be too helpful. It was not the caretaker's job to deal with drunken Headmasters.

Especially if he's just fired you.

Neither was it in Jack's contract. But he had a sympathy for drunks. Poor saps conducting nightly suicides. In goes the poison, until the lights go out. Death of the mind, of responsibility, of fear and failure. He'd heard it all at his alcohol group, his semi-survivors' group. The analysis of their degradation. With waking up came the comeuppance. The vomiting, the awful headaches, the shame, though it was surprising how quickly you put it out of mind. Or why would anyone go through that again?

He'd have to take him home.

How? Jack could hardly drag him. Drive him? But the effort of dragging him to the van, getting him inside, and getting him out the other end... Forget it. He had a wheelbarrow in the van. A somewhat undignified means of conveyance, but a drunken stupor hardly warranted a gold coach.

Leaving the Headmaster, Jack went out to the car park. He opened the back of his van and took out his wheelbarrow. And with it, a couple of painting sheets to cushion the metal.

And wheeled it back into the school.

The Head was heavy, an unhelpful, dead weight. Cumbrously, Jack lifted him in the barrow. And then shifted him so his weight was evenly distributed, head facing Jack at the front, his legs dangling over the back between the handles.

Jack pushed his passenger out of the school, and along the path to the big house. He was a weight, but Jack had pushed heavier ones in this same wheelbarrow and over rougher terrain. This path had paving flagstones or bitumen all the way.

He was about to turn into the drive of the house when George, the caretaker, saw him from the front garden of the gatehouse. Noting the load, he came striding up.

'Drunk,' said Jack.

'And there's me hoping he'd be dead,' exclaimed George. He bent down and looked into the headmaster's face, and grimaced at the alcohol smell. 'You drunken slob,' he went on. 'You deserve to be dead for what you're doing to me and my family. I hate your bloody guts. You lowlife stinker!'

'Feel better for that?' said Jack.

'Lots,' grinned George. And spat in the headmaster's face.

Jack pushed him away.

'That was uncalled for, George.'

The caretaker nodded. 'Sorry. That was a bit much. But I am in such a fury... And all from that old prick.'

'I know how you feel,' said Jack. 'Just don't do it. He won't see it or feel it, anyway. So there isn't any point.'

Jack took out a grubby tissue, shrugged, and wiped the phlegm off the Head's cheek.

George held his hands up. 'You're right, Jack. Keep it to yourself. He isn't worth my spit. Take him home and dump him in the bath.'

Jack left him. The caretaker stood watching a while as Jack wheeled his load along the path. Then George headed back to his house. He was not going to help carry the drunk in.

At the big house, Jack left the wheelbarrow at the foot of the steps, went up them and rang the doorbell. He wondered at the reception he was going to get, bringing a drunken headmaster home in a wheelbarrow. Would he get thanked or cursed?

Ellie opened the door.

'Hello, Jack,' she said, obviously surprised.

Jack indicated his load at the foot of the few steps.

'I found your dad, dead drunk in the school corridor.'

Ellie sighed. 'Oh how shameful.' She came down the stairs to look at him. 'Daddy, Daddy, this is terrible. How could you?'

Jack had nothing to say. He shouldn't be a witness.

'We'd best bring him in,' she said.

Jack took his legs and arms, she took his feet. And they carried him up the stairs, and into the wide, dark wood hallway, past various portraits Jack had no opportunity to closely inspect. And was directed into a side room, where Cathy and her mother were drinking coffee.

'He's drunk,' said Ellie, struggling with her half of her comatose father. 'The builder here found him in the school corridor. And brought him over.'

Her mother vacated the sofa.

'Put him there, please,' she said.

Cathy moved the coffee table to make more room. And they dumped him on the sofa. Vicky put a cushion under his head.

'Thank you very much, young man,' said Vicky. 'I'm sorry to put you to this trouble.'

'I couldn't leave him in the hallway, madam.'

'No,' she said. 'Thank you for being so thoughtful. One moment.'

She went to her handbag.

'It's alright...' Jack began. Not that he couldn't do with it. But pride said take nothing.

She took out twenty pounds.

'I can't accept it,' said Jack, holding up his hands. 'I did what anyone would.'

'Take it,' ordered Cathy.

He was surprised at her harshness, and hesitated.

Cathy hurriedly took the note from her mother and pushed it into Jack's hand.

'We are grateful,' she said coldly.

Jack looked at the money. There was no doubt he needed it. He eyed the harsh face of the woman who stood in front of him, clearly dismissing him. He was on the verge of throwing the twenty back at her, but hesitated too long. And instead pocketed the note.

Ellie saw him to the door.

'I'm sorry about the tip,' she said. 'My family are like that. We have to tip. It is expected of us.'

'I certainly wasn't after it,' he said, knowing that taking the tip put him in his place. As if he hadn't done the task out of human decency but in the hope of a gratuity.

She kissed him on the cheek.

'Thank you, Jack.'

He smiled and she back at him. That was worth more than the twenty quid. Then again, a twenty was a twenty. A kiss wouldn't put food on the table.

PART TWO:
THE FIRST MURDER

Chapter 14

'What must that builder think of us?' said Vicky.

She was seated in an armchair, Cathy had the other. Ellie was seated on one of the dining chairs. Their father lay sprawled out on the sofa on his back, mouth agape, one arm dangling down the side of the sofa. His jacket lay wanly open, as if he'd prepared for his spree like a man out on the town. His watch held in its snug pocket in spite of its owner's travails.

Cathy flapped a hand. 'The builder's of no consequence. But think, if it had been a parent who had found him. Or even a student.' Her hand slapped her cheek at the disgrace.

'Horror,' said Vicky. She had got up and buttoned up her husband's jacket, straightened the collar, as if a parent were due.

'Why does Daddy do it?' said Ellie feebly.

'Because even he knows what's happening to this school,' said Vicky wiping her husband's face with a tissue, 'but vainly hopes a fairy godmother will fly in at the last moment. And you can only believe that half cut.'

'Shall I get him a blanket?' said Ellie, standing with her mother over her father, his head fallen into his chest as if he couldn't look at them, his mouth wide open.

'He's not cold,' said Cathy. 'And sod him if he is.'

'A rubber sheet might be better, dear,' said Vicky. She was peering at her husband closely, feeling his cheek and brow. He rolled over and groaned. 'I think he's already wet himself,' she added. 'Though luckily not here.'

'I'll get something,' said Ellie, and left them.

'It's like being at a funeral,' sighed Cathy. 'The corpse in a coffin on trestles. The mourners, making small talk.'

Vicky gave a tight smile. 'Graham always was a scene stealer.'

'Here lies the Head of a middle ranking independent school,' said Cathy, behind the sofa looking down on her father. 'Note the control, the firm hand on the tiller. I'm sure Ellie would find a better metaphor... Here lies the sodden man who hands out the prizes on Speech Day, the cups for athletics and hockey, who leads us in prayer in assembly... The man who has sold us for thirty pieces of silver.'

Ellie returned with a large plastic sheet.

'This is the best I could find,' she said.

'That'll do,' said Vicky, taking the sheet from her. 'Get him off the sofa.'

Ellie and Cathy took an end each and lifted their father to the carpet.

'Oh he's shat himself,' grimaced Cathy, shaking her contaminated hands. 'It's dripping down his leg.'

Ellie gave a faint smile, glad she'd taken the other end. Vicky tucked in the plastic sheet all around the seating of the sofa.

'Put him back,' she said.

'I'm not holding him by his legs again,' said Cathy.

'Do it while your hands are shitty,' said Vicky. 'Then wash them.'

'Why do I always get the dirty jobs?'

Ellie said nothing. Shit on her sister's fingers said it for her. They lifted their father back onto the sofa, over the plastic sheet, and laid him down. Immediately done, Cathy rushed out of the room making yucky sounds, hands held out in front of her.

'He does smell somewhat,' said Ellie.

'It's one thing wiping a baby's bottom,' said Vicky wearily, 'or even a pair of them. You expect that. And everything's to hand. But it's not quite the same with a grown man.'

'At least he doesn't know anything,' said Ellie.

'Doesn't want to know,' said Vicky. 'Isn't that the trouble? No matter what mess he makes, it's his womenfolk who will clean up after him.'

Cathy re-entered, still grimacing.

'That was a disgusting job.'

The three of them sat down. There were things to be said. A future to be sorted out. He was their focus, the silent fourth, a reminder to keep them on track. Every so often he wriggled and thrashed on the plastic which squeaked under him. And settled back to some temporary comfort, before sparking synapses demanded another twist and thrash.

'He's in a coma, isn't he?' said Cathy. 'Oblivious to pissing and shitting himself. To his own stink. To the state of Bramley.'

'We won't get a better chance,' said Vicky.

They looked to her, alerted by the tone and train.

'Bramley doesn't have long,' she went on. 'Weeks. Lady Margaret won't be able to give us a leaseback once the school is in receivership. We can't wait.'

'It would be child's play to smash his brains in,' said Cathy, raising a fist as if to do so.

'And we'd all end up in prison,' said Ellie. 'A murdered father, husband, Head of Bramley, with a head smashed in, on our sofa, in our front room. Smart thinking, Cathy.'

'It has to be an accident,' said Vicky sucking her lower lip thoughtfully. 'He's drunk. So, poor man, he falls into the lake and drowns.'

'You mean we throw him in,' exclaimed Ellie.

'I mean he falls in, a drunken stupor,' said Vicky, matter of fact. 'Stumbles about the lake, drinking all day, then a splash. And oops, a complete accident. Found in the morning. Oh dear. Sympathy from the world. Funeral.

'Everyone in black. Lots of flowers. Tributes. I take over as Head, Lady Margaret completes the formalities of the leaseback. And all's right with the world.'

'Except we'd have drowned Daddy,' said Ellie.

'Oh dear,' mocked Cathy, 'the poor thing has her scruples. She'd prefer to be broke on her way to sainthood.'

'I am not quite the eager murderess you are, Cathy.'

'Daddy's favourite wouldn't be,' she laughed, automatically straightening her skirt. 'Protector of the shitty man. The house gone, the school gone, the grounds pulled away... Never mind all the running about and effort we've put in as a family... Here come the bailiffs to put us out on the street.'

Ellie was standing over her father, a hand on his shoulder. He flapped an arm as if to brush her away, groaned and rolled onto his face.

'Daddy, why have you done this to us?'

'Shit and piss is your answer,' scorned Cathy. 'To every sensible question. Faeces and vomit. But his daughter with the First feels pity. Wasted on him. Stupid of her. Don't you think, Daddy? You preferred classics and literature to the hard things in life. Science and mathematics were always too practical for you.'

'Which is why she wants to kill you.'

Cathy rose, on the other side of the sofa to Ellie. She looked down at their father.

'You want to walk hand in hand with him to the poor house, Ellie,' she said. 'You'll be his Little Dorrit, his faithful lapdog. Running errands barefoot, out there with the begging bowl... Oh, I'm weeping already for sweet Ellie.'

Ellie closed her eyes. She could smell alcohol and faeces and pee, as well as her sister's disdain.

'He's still your father, Cathy,' she said wearily. 'Whatever else, your father. You have half his genes. There's some science for you.'

'And if my genes are to survive,' said Cathy, twisting her father's nose, 'what must I do to his?'

'You have already decided,' exclaimed Ellie.

'I once promised to love, honour and obey,' said Vicky, shuffling as she looked down on her husband. 'And I've kept my part up to now. More than kept it. But he promised in his turn to keep me, not to sell his birthright for a mess of pottage.'

'You're mixing up your Bible stories, Mummy,' said Ellie.

'I did my duty, he did not do his,' she said ignoring her. 'So I must take over.' She turned to them both. 'I am your mother. I have a responsibility for the two of you. For the family.'

The prone man groaned, thrashed an arm against the sofa back, and pulled himself into a foetal ball.

'You have both decided,' declared Ellie. 'I can see that. And I see the sense of it. But...'

'But Bramley,' said her mother, an arm on her shoulder. 'If we hesitate we'll go down with his ship.'

Ellie might have objected to her mother's tumble of metaphors, if this were an essay. But she wasn't marking, her hand on her father's shoulder, her mother's on hers. Her father was too much to bear. Her mother's demand was impossible. She wanted to be somewhere else. Some other, cleaner, happier world.

'Think, Ellie. How much longer can he last?' said Cathy. She had taken a step back from the sofa as if to keep the fumes off her suit. 'His heart, his drinking... Suppose he dies in six months time. Dissolute. And everything is gone. Oh, the waste of it!'

'This is awful,' exclaimed Ellie, her hands to her face. 'We are ghouls.'

'Then leave it to me and Mummy,' said Cathy. 'You go to the cinema and stay holy.'

Ellie got down on one knee and cupped her father's cheeks. His face was warm, she could smell the liquor intermingled with the animal odours. She fingered his moustache, something she had liked to do as a child, as if it were a pet.

'Forgive me,' she whispered. 'There is no other way, Daddy.' And turned to her mother. 'What have we got to do?'

'Make sure he stays drunk,' she said. She turned away from them. 'One minute.'

Vicky left the room.

'I knew you'd come round,' said Cathy gently. 'A half share of nothing is still nothing.'

'I've not murdered anyone before,' she said, aware of her breathing in the quiet of the room.

'You think I have?'

'You seem more practised.'

Cathy smiled. 'I'm a practical person, Ellie. Science is experimental. Besides, living to simply exist is amoeboid. We are DeNeuves. All this.' She gestured around her, at the antique furniture, at the portraits on the walls. 'What are we without it?'

'We're afraid to find out.'

Vicky returned. She was carrying a length of tubing and a funnel.

'Bring me the whisky,' she ordered Cathy.

Cathy went to the cabinet and brought over a mostly full bottle. Vicky fitted the funnel into the tubing.

'Hold him in a seated position,' she said.

Ellie took one side, Cathy the other. They lifted their father until he was upright against the back of the sofa.

'Keep a hold on him,' said Vicky.

She pushed her husband's head back and opened his mouth as wide as she could. And then began feeding in the tubing, inch by inch down his throat, into his gullet, and further. Choking sounds came from him, but she persevered. They ceased and she continued, until there was only a few inches of tubing outside his mouth, the funnel at its end.

Vicky took the stopper off the bottle and poured the liquid slowly into the funnel. The whisky gurgled out and down the tube. They could hear and feel its hollow journey. When the funnel was empty, she refilled it, her daughters holding their father upright.

'Not so quickly,' said Cathy, staying her mother's arm. 'Or he might sick it all up. Give him a few minutes before the next wallop.'

They stood, they waited, Vicky holding the half full bottle. No one spoke for half a minute or more. She looked to her daughters as if awaiting a signal, shrugged and poured in more whisky. The liquid burbled and jumped as it struggled to exit via the small orifice of the funnel. Into the tubing, a stream of clear brown poison, twisting down his gullet and into the pool of his stomach.

'Keep him upright,' said Cathy, holding his shoulder firmly. 'Gravity will keep the alcohol down until it's absorbed.'

'Science has the answer,' said Ellie. 'Would you like to give us a commentary on what is going on in his belly?'

'I studied maths and physics. Not chemistry.'

'He is getting pickled,' said Vicky, slowly pouring the dregs of the bottle. 'Your father will be preserved for years to come.'

Chapter 15

Jack watched them come through the barrier. Good job he'd had the twenty that he'd almost thrown back at them, as he'd had to get petrol at Romford. That was fifteen gone. And he'd had to park fifteen minutes' walk away. He'd better get some money on account for this job tomorrow. It was a thirty mile drive out to Billericay every day. And his car drank petrol as if there were a hole in the tank.

Mia had a small suitcase on wheels. He thought how much she looked like her mother, who had no luggage. The same chestnut hair, and Mia, already quite tall for her age, would likely be as tall as her mother in a few years. Alison frowned as she saw him. He knew that face of old. She would have been quite happy for him to drive to Brighton and then back again in an evening. Shamefully, he'd pleaded poverty. Though he might have made it with the £20 tip, but whether he'd have got back home was a moot point.

He crossed the station concourse to meet them.

'Hello, Alison. Hello, Mia.'

'Hi, Dad.'

'Hello, Jack.' She looked at the departure board and pressed her lips. 'There's a train leaving in 20 minutes. I'd like to catch it back. Just time for a coffee.'

They walked en famille to the coffee bar with Mia between her parents. He still had a five pound note, he could offer to pay for himself. But then again, he had to get back to Billericay tomorrow. Hold on to it. He might well need it.

'What do you want, Jack?'

'Just a filter coffee,' he said.

'Find a table. I'll get the drinks.'

He did as he was bid. Mia went with her mother to fuss over her choice of drink and what to have with it. The table was full of dirty cups and plates. Jack gathered them together and put them on another table. Then sat down, spacing himself out by putting his bag on one of the seats and Mia's suitcase by the other.

He'd be glad when Alison was away, so he could have time with Mia without the refrain of a soured history. Sometimes it seemed they were heading for friendship, and then a blow up out of nothing and she'd remind him of past transgressions. It was her revenge. When their relationship was breaking up, when he was drunk more often than not – and she was in effect a single parent, but more than just of Mia. Still, he just had to hold tight for fifteen minutes. Be sociable.

She'd be a murderous teacher, he thought. Any kid sent to her, the deputy head, would know they'd better improve or else they'd be back. But she was going into hospital, he remembered somewhat guiltily. He was curious what for. The fact that she was not saying suggested it could be serious. Some woman's thing, she'd said. Whatever that meant.

They came over to the table, Alison carrying the tray of drinks. And sat down. Alison handed out the coffees and Mia's frothy orange drink with a straw.

'I hope it's not serious,' he said carefully. 'Your hospital thing.'

'Me too,' she said, and surreptitiously indicated Mia.

Which he took to mean she might have told him if Mia wasn't there. And as she was, he would not be told.

'I'll be in for a couple of days,' she said. 'You can bring Mia back Thursday evening.'

Oh heavens, worse than he thought. He'd hoped it was an overnight stay. How was he going to manage things? He'd take Mia to the school tomorrow, but she'd be bored stiff if she had to stay for more than a day at Bramley. If he worked like hell tomorrow, he might be able to finish the job. Then have a couple of days off. There was a small job he had lined up but he'd have to delay till next week. If he could.

'Here's £40,' she said. And she laid two 20s on the table.

'I am working,' he said belittled, 'it's just I'm awaiting payment...'

'Just take them,' she said.

She sounded just like that DeNeuve woman. He'd half a mind to leave them there. But Mia needed feeding and so forth. And so he took the notes, screwing them up in his pocket.

'I'll pay you back,' he said.

'Forget it,' she said.

And he knew it was serious. She could so easily have taken his lack of cash and hit him with it. But she hadn't.

'What we doing tomorrow, Dad?'

'Well, I'm working at this really nice school,' he said. 'Big grounds, woodlands, a lake, playing fields, lots of computers, a library full of books and films...'

'Independent, is it?' said Alison.

'Yes,' he admitted. Alison was political about such things. Felt the private sector robbed the state sector. He would normally have agreed with anyone who intimated such thoughts, but now it was Alison and he needed to justify himself, so he scrambled for reasons.

But Alison left it. And he knew for certain something was really worrying her.

'Can we go out with the telescope tonight, Dad?' said Mia.

'Don't see why not.'

'Don't be up too late,' said Alison.

'It's school holidays, Mum.'

'Looking forward to your new school?' he said to Mia.

'I don't know,' she said, screwing up her face. 'Could be brilliant. Could be horrible.'

'Probably won't be brilliant or horrible,' he said.

'A couple of friends from school are going too,' she said thoughtfully. 'So I'll have some protection.'

'What?' he said, 'from the Mafia?'

'You gotta have a gang,' said Mia, 'or they'll pick on you.'

He didn't know who he was most worried about, his ex or his daughter.

'How do you know this?' he said.

'I've heard,' she said mysteriously.

Alison rolled her eyes. 'We've been through this a dozen times. She thinks the school is all bullies and sadistic teachers.' She looked at her watch. 'Now I must go.' She kissed Mia. 'Be good. And I'll see you Thursday. Bye, Jack.'

'Hope it goes well,' he called after her.

And watched her as she left the café and went out onto the concourse.

'Breast cancer,' said Mia quietly.

'How do you know?'

'I heard her talking on the phone. And saw her crying.'

'Is she having an operation?'

'What's a biopsy?' said Mia.

'I don't know.'

'Well she said that to someone. And an op or something.'

He thought some more. 'Probably means tests,' he said with a shrug. 'And if they find something, well...' He stopped, beyond the limits of his knowledge. 'Could be more. I don't know.'

She was thoughtful, gurgling the bubbles at the bottom of her glass.

'Anyway,' he said, 'let's get you back, if we are going to go stargazing tonight.'

Chapter 16

Jenny and George were in their youngest son's room. There were posters round the room of super heroes, there were empty drawers on the bare mattress on the bedsprings. Jenny was emptying further drawers from a chest of drawers, first onto the bed and then putting the contents into large, blue plastic bags. George was on his knees filling a cardboard box with books from the bookshelf.

'We've got far too much,' he said wearily. 'I don't know how we'll fit it all in.'

'Could we leave some here? For a week or two,' said his wife. 'They're not going to sell the house that quick.'

'I can't stomach asking him,' said George.

'You must.'

'Jack wheeled him up to his house, you should've seen him – laid out like a dead pig in the wheelbarrow. I can't get over that. He'd pissed himself. Utterly out to the world. What a state!'

'I'd have spat in his eye,' she said.

'What's the point when he doesn't know?' he said uncomfortably.

'Stupid and childish it might be,' she said, emptying another drawer. 'But quite satisfying. Will you ask?'

'I'll have to.' He looked wearily about the room, at their demolition. 'Every time I see him, I want to snap at him, tell him exactly what I think of him. But I have to be on best behaviour, as if all we ever wanted was to be sacked and lose the house.'

'You'll need his reference,' she said. 'Don't blow it, George.'

'Bastard.'

'What about the service company's offer?' she said.

'What? Come back here for ten thousand a year less? Watch someone move into this house...'

'A stopgap,' she said. 'It'll be some money coming in.'

'And see them DeNeuves every day...' He sat on the bed. 'It'd be so humiliating. They think they're so much better than us. Born to lord it. They push us about like we're sheep they can send to the slaughter whenever they snap their fingers.'

Jenny sat on the bed.

'That Cathy DeNeuve has so much swank,' she said. 'She cuts me dead, unless it's to tell me off.' She turned to her husband. 'What is it with these people? Why do they think they have the right?'

'The next job I go for,' he said. 'A state school. No more of this top drawer snobbery. I'll join the union, get some respect.'

'I remember when we first came here,' said Jenny, closing her eyes and wiping the lids. 'I couldn't believe it was all going to be ours. Before the boys were born... All these rooms, so many cupboards, the garden, the view over the playing fields and the lake...' She sniffed, holding back a tear. 'We've been spoilt here, George. But it was never ours.' She sighed and shook her head. 'I do hope the next person looks after my garden.' She wiped her eye with the back of her hand. 'It's no good thinking like that. It was never ours. This was always on the cards right from day one.'

George held her hand and squeezed it.

'And here we are removing every scrap of evidence that we've ever lived here,' he said. 'So depressing. Packing seventeen years into boxes. And then taking them to the new place... Boxes, bloody boxes.'

'It's only temporary, George.'

'So we're going to be doing this again in a few months?'

She shrugged. 'What else can we do?'

He stood up. 'Let's leave it for tonight. We've done too much already. And I can't face any more. And you're knackered too.'

She nodded. 'Yeh. That'll do for today. Get going again, first thing in the morning.'

'I'm going to take the dog out. His nightly walk round the estate. I'm sure he thinks I own it. And he has no idea in his soppy head that he's going to lose it all.'

'And the kids,' she said. 'They won't be coming back here. Straight to the new place. Won't that be a come down for 'em.'

'Don't start me off,' he said. 'But you know, now there's no choice, it'll be a relief to get away from here. To get on with life, wherever we are, and stop moaning. Sod the DeNeuves. They don't own the world. It'll be a blessing to see the last of them.'

Chapter 17

Cathy drove her car to the gate of the big house. She didn't lock up but left all the car doors wide open, before coming up the path to the porch where Vicky and Ellie were waiting. They'd managed to drag Mr DeNeuve outside. He lay untidily splayed out on the porch, mouth open, hair awry, his breathing almost inaudible, apart from the occasional sigh.

The two women were exhausted from their efforts. Dribbles of faeces lay on the hall carpet. Ellie sniffed her hands. This was a dirty business.

'How are we ever going to get him to the car?' said Vicky.

'He came here by wheelbarrow...' said Ellie.

'I'll go get mine then,' said Vicky. And went round the side of the house.

The sun had set. There was a red hue through the trees over the lake. Shadows had gone. There were no stars in a grey sky streaked with charcoal. I will wash everything before I go to bed tonight, thought Ellie. Scrub myself all over.

'Are you still game?' said Cathy.

'I am one minute,' said Ellie. 'Not the next.'

'Can you contemplate losing this?' Her arm swept across the playing fields, along the trees and lake.

'No.'

'Keep it to the fore,' said Cathy.

Their mother came round the house with the wheelbarrow. It was less substantial than Jack's, built for lesser weights, for less strong users. She stopped at the edge of the steps, the barrow waiting for its load.

They dragged and rolled Mr DeNeuve down the steps sideways, and managed to get him in the wheelbarrow. He was face down, almost like a dead fish, his head poking out the front as if watching the wheel, his legs between the handles, the black shoes mucky. Cathy took one handle, Ellie the other and they pushed him along the path to the gate.

'Keep off the flowers,' said Vicky.

'It's not easy,' complained Cathy as the two of them bumped along the path, trying not to touch each other and to keep off the side flower beds.

Once outside the gate, Ellie went in the car from the far door, crawled over the seat and took her father's arms and head. Cathy pushed from behind, grimacing as she had to grip his shoes and ankles. As he came further in, Ellie got under his armpits and dragged. She stumbled and fell over his chest, her hands landing in the wetness of his groin. Shower, soap, shampoo for a week, she thought. She gave a last haul, let go, and her father fell off the seat, into the gully.

'Leave him there,' said Cathy. 'I don't want his mess on the seat.'

'Take the wheelbarrow with,' said Vicky.

They put it on the backseat just above Mr DeNeuve, and the three sat in the front. Cathy's car had been chosen as it was the roomiest, with four doors and room for three front and back. They all sat in the front, Vicky in the middle, Ellie by the passenger door and Cathy driving. Ellie automatically went to put her seatbelt on before stopping herself. This was a slow drive without traffic.

Cathy had the lights on low, driving barely above walking pace as if this were a car in a cortege on the way to a cemetery. The occupants were silent, they knew where they were going, they knew what they were going to do.

Ellie looked behind her. The wheelbarrow was on the seat. She couldn't see her father laid out in his ditch, but could smell the sweet, shitty smell which she felt must be all over her. And deserved to be. She thought of the alcohol they had poured into their father, adding to the amount he'd drunk himself. They were poisoners. They would be worse, she thought, as the car glided down the hill along the line of trees. She could stop them. Perhaps. And regret forever. Perhaps. But the car was running, her mother and sister with her.

It wasn't done, till it was over. Like Hamlet watching his uncle at prayer. More hesitation, worry about consequences. Heaven and Hell. The car rode on. She closed her eyes. It was a short journey, the whole family here.

Cathy stopped the car about five metres from the lake. The water was choppy and as dark grey as the cloud above. Three honking geese homed in and skimmed across the surface, wings drawing in as they lowered to lake level, the drag of the water catching their feet and slowing them until they were floating.

Ellie got out of the car. It had grown chilly, she wasn't dressed for an evening by the lake, her arms goosepimply. Cathy in her suit was warmer, but her semi high heels not quite right for the task ahead of them. As if they had both come to the wrong party. Mother wore a sensible sweater and flat, sensible shoes.

'Get the wheelbarrow out, Ellie.'

She did so, in machine mode, barely thinking ahead. She left it at the car door. Then she went round the other side of the vehicle to push her father out as Cathy, over the wheelbarrow, dragged at his legs until he was in the bowl of it. Ellie came round to join her, and the two of them pushed and pulled until he was better placed in the barrow.

They took a breather. A half moon glowed in the clouds. Their father lay face up like a manikin, arms, legs and arms splayed over the side of the barrow. The extra alcohol had done its work. He was a lump of flesh and bone, living you might say, with as much feeling as a sack of potatoes.

'Let's get this over with,' said Cathy.

She took one of the handles, Ellie the other, and they pushed the wheelbarrow slowly to the water's edge. As they got closer the ground became softer and muddier, and the wheelbarrow made a track with its single rubber wheel and became harder to push.

They stopped at the edge of the lake, breathing heavily.

'Do you want to say a prayer?' said Cathy.

'Don't be stupid.'

Cathy laughed. 'We're in this together, Ellie. There's no backing out. Daddy is in a wheelbarrow, utterly paralytic, and we are about to tip him in the lake.'

'Then we are both stupid.'

She caressed her father's cheek. It was warm with bristles growing through. She could still walk away. Having filled him with liquor, having barrowed him to the lake... She could turn away and leave it to her mother and sister.

But it would still be done. With her or without her, he would be killed.

'I'm getting cold,' said Cathy. 'Let's finish this.'

Ellie joined her at the side of the wheelbarrow. They tipped it sideways and Mr DeNeuve fell out into a few inches of ebbing water. Once settled, he lay face up, almost as if sleeping. Ellie was tempted to do up the other buttons of his jacket as he would do himself before an assembly. Cathy stepped into the water and beckoned to her sister. And the two of them rolled him over and over, until he was in deeper water and lying face down.

The sisters came out of the lake, their shoes wet and muddy with splatters about their legs, their feet icy cold.

Their father lay like a long island a few feet off the shore, the water bobbing about his half submerged ears, his hair wet and mud streaked.

Might he yet turn himself over, thought Ellie, as a border collie ran splashing into the water.

They turned. And saw George coming in rapidly. Vicky was leaning on the car bonnet. George stopped once he was beyond the car, and looked at the three of them, the muddy legs of the daughters, the upturned wheelbarrow, the new island in the water. He switched on his torch, though it was barely needed, and shone it on the headmaster, bobbing facedown in the shallows.

'What are you up to?' said George.

'What do you think?' said Vicky.

Ellie could almost hear the ticking of his brain as he attempted to make sense of the tableau.

'This isn't a rescue,' he said.

He walked up to the wheelbarrow lying on its side, and stared at the headmaster facedown in the lake. Ellie waited for him to say the obvious.

'You were drowning him.'

And felt relief. Now someone else could take over. It would no longer be the prerogative of her family.

'Are you going to save him, George?' said Cathy.

He was at the edge of the lake between the two daughters, the water inches from his shoes, all focused on the half floating headmaster. The border collie came to his side and he grabbed him by the collar and snapped the lead on. He looked at the three women in turn.

'You know what this is?'

'We do,' said Cathy. 'Are you going to pull him out?'

George took a step back with his dog.

'After what he's done to me?' He looked to Vicky, she hadn't moved from her resting point on the car bonnet.

'What do you want, George?' she said.

He scratched his head and turned his back on the lake, as if in that movement he'd made his decision.

'If I get my job back,' he said to Vicky, 'then I've seen nothing. If I get my house back, I was never here.'

'Agreed,' said Vicky.

He looked to the two daughters. Cathy shrugged indicating her helplessness. Ellie nodded.

'Come on, boy,' said George, tugging at the lead. 'We'll go for a walk round the school. Then home.'

They watched him head up the hill. He did not turn, and was soon between the trees and lost to them in the shadows.

Chapter 18

Jack and Mia had driven out to Barn Hill by Epping Forest. The sun had set half an hour ago, leaving a long summer twilight barely quelled by the time the sun is ready to rise once more. They'd set up the telescope in the hope that the cloud would break. The lights of the city were a few miles away, beyond the farm lane and reservoir. This was a high point, a good viewing spot. On clear nights.

They were on a bench eating pizza. Jack had brought his thermos and two cups. The two of them were dressed for a night of observing with scarves, woolly hats and fingerless gloves.

'There's not a single star,' said Mia dismally.

'It's getting worse,' he said. 'There were a few open patches when we left home, but now even they've gone.'

'I wanted to see Jupiter and Mars,' she said.

Before leaving Forest Gate they had looked in his astronomy magazine. And both planets were well positioned tonight. Mia knew the names of the four large Jupiter moons and had brought pencils and sketchbook to draw a picture of the gas giant.

'I am so disappointed,' she said. 'I was looking forward to it as me and Mum were coming up by train. Watching the sky, thinking it'll probably be OK. And it might even get better. Instead it's got worse.'

'Sorry,' he said, as if it were his fault.

She concentrated on her pizza, he on his tea. He would of course have liked it to be clear up here, but it wasn't a bad place for a picnic and a chat. It wasn't cold, and he was well used to the vagaries of the English skies. His philosophy was practical; expect the night sky to be cloudy, and from time to time you get a pleasant surprise.

'Do people die of breast cancer?' she said.

He hadn't brought up this topic earlier and wondered how long before she did. To test his ignorance.

'We don't know that she's got it,' he said, which of course wasn't an answer. And added, 'If they catch it early then most people survive.'

He was pretty certain that was true. That was the way it was with most cancers, get it early, cut it out. Maybe radium treatment, maybe chemotherapy. But he was floundering. His knowledge of cancer was limited. Not so long ago it wasn't talked about at all or in euphemisms. The dreaded 'C word' and the like. And of course, people did die of it. But for the who, the when, the how – you don't normally ask a builder.

'If she dies, then I'll have to come and live with you.'

'She's not dying.'

'I was just saying...'

'Well, don't kill your mum off just yet.'

He was finding this doubly, triply, uncomfortable. There was his ignorance, there was an eleven year old. There was his future and Mia's if she died. Which she wasn't going to do. But if, how would he manage with an eleven year old to look after?

'She won't talk about it,' she said.

And he knew it had to be serious, as you would talk about it if it was trivial. If it was just tests. And he felt angry at Alison for keeping them in the dark. She wasn't on her own. There were others to be considered. Then again, he wondered whether he would talk. Say, bowel cancer or, more embarrassingly, testicular. The human body had its surprises.

'Let's assume it's not very much,' he said.

'Why?'

He wanted to say because it's easier, but he couldn't. It wasn't an answer but a fob off. A pushing away of harder truths.

'Because we don't know,' he said. 'Because your mum is still young. 36 is young, relatively speaking. Her health's been good up to now. And let's hope they've found it early.'

'And if they haven't?'

'Let's hope they have.'

He needed a serious chat with Alison, as soon as she was out of hospital. To know where they were both going as parents. He occasionally wondered whether it would have been better to be childless. And the different life he'd now be living. If Mia wasn't conceived twelve years ago. But it wasn't really a consideration. He was here, where he was, with an eleven year old daughter. With no plans to kill her off.

'A star,' he said, pointing to a space in the carapace. 'Could that be Jupiter?'

Mia peered at the lone star. 'It's in the wrong place. And it's gone.'

'Let's pack up,' he said. 'No viewing tonight. A dud.'

'What we doing tomorrow?' she said.

'I'll take you into the school where I'm working. It's got a library, loads of computers, playing fields and a beautiful lake with swans and ducks.'

'That sounds amazing.'

Chapter 19

The big house was a flurry of activity. Immediately she'd got in, Ellie put all her clothes in the washing machine, including her trainers which she put into a pillow case, and wandered about barefoot and naked under a dressing gown. Cathy, a little slower, was peeved she'd missed out on the washing machine, but on reflection went for hand cleaning of her shoes, tights and skirt. Any mud, faeces, all traces of their expedition she scrubbed vigorously away. Vicky hosed out the wheelbarrow and washed the plastic sheet that had lain on the sofa. She crawled over the carpet searching for tiny drippings, soaping and watering them away.

Ellie grabbed the shower first. The others followed. And at last all three sat in dressing gowns, drinking hot chocolate in the sitting room.

'He's well and truly dead now,' said Cathy.

'Shut up,' exclaimed Ellie.

'We might as well get used to the pattern of the rest of our lives, Ellie.'

'I'm not proud of what we did, Cathy.' She raised her palms to stop Cathy saying why she should be. 'But I understand the necessity. It's just, I'd rather you didn't crow.'

'I am not crowing, but the future has happened.'

'How banal.'

'Shut up the pair of you,' said Vicky. 'Let's think where we are.'

'Here, drinking hot cocoa as if nothing has happened,' said Ellie.

'Oh, that damned caretaker!' exclaimed Cathy. 'Catching us like that. I almost jumped out of my skin when I saw that dog.'

'I saw him coming,' said Vicky. 'There was nothing I could do.'

'He caught us in the act,' said Ellie. 'Daddy facedown, wheelbarrow on its side, and our muddy shoes and legs. He had us bang to rights.'

'Another few minutes and we'd have been gone,' said Vicky.

'Then he might have found Daddy and dragged him out...' said Cathy. 'Mouth to mouth and all that. And the corpse might have come to life.'

'Not the worst of outcomes,' said Ellie.

Cathy held up her hands. 'Don't get me started.'

'The caretaker forced us into making a deal,' said Vicky.

'We do need a caretaker,' said Ellie.

'Do we need that one?' said Cathy.

'We do for the time being,' mused Vicky. 'Let him have his job back, his house. Keep him quiet. Besides which, he's implicated anyway. For how can he say he saw us, without admitting he left your father in the lake himself.'

'I don't like having him around,' said Cathy.

'Well, say, this term, we keep him on,' said Vicky. 'Once the autopsy is all over, and your father is cremated... Then we can give him notice.'

'He could still talk,' said Cathy.

'Unlikely,' said her mother. 'And if he did, who'd believe a caretaker who'd been given notice? And I dare say we can find some bad workmanship to make him look simply vindictive.'

'Can't we simply leave him in his job?' said Ellie. 'Fulfil our part of the bargain.'

'And face him every day for the next twenty years?' said Cathy. 'Knowing he knows what he knows.'

Ellie had no response. She didn't think George and his family deserved loss of job and home. But this was her family. Her legacy. And George had seen the unseeable.

'This room is clean,' said Vicky. 'I've done the carpet, wheelbarrow, all our clothes have been in the machine...'

'One of us needs to look at the garden path when it's daylight,' said Cathy.

'And your car,' said Ellie.

'Oh, what a stink shop! I'll do it first thing in the morning...'

'One other thing,' said Vicky. 'A priority. The wheelbarrow tyre-prints by the lake...'

'Oh God,' said Ellie. 'What on earth are we going to do about them?'

'Scrape them away,' said Cathy.

'When?' said Vicky. 'And who?'

'I am not going down to that lake,' said Ellie. 'Oh no!'

'Are you volunteering me, sister dear?' said Cathy.

'I am not going down there.'

'One of us has to.'

'Not me.'

'He is well and truly dead,' said Cathy.

'Oh shut up, you grave snatcher.'

They were silent a while. Ellie thinking of the tyre-prints and too many footprints by the lake where they'd done their work. All too close to their father's body. Could she do it? Erase them. But she'd just washed all her clothes. And her father would be floating there, accusing. In daylight maybe... but at one in the morning?

'I've got my car to do,' said Cathy, 'so it's not fair if I have to clean up the lakeside too.'

'It has to be done now,' said Vicky. 'Right away.'

'Why?' said Ellie.

'Who knows what will happen in the morning,' she said. 'We must clean that area before anyone comes. And it has to be one of you two doing it.'

Ellie looked at Cathy who smirked back at her, knowing she could do it, but why should she?

'I'll toss you for it,' said Ellie grimly.

'I don't have to do it,' said Cathy with a sigh, 'but one of us has to. So, OK. A single toss. And I'm heads.'

'Mummy to toss.'

Vicky went to her handbag and sorted out a coin. She put down the bag, and placed the coin over her thumb and first finger. 'Ready?' she said to them both. 'I'm not much good at this, so you'll have to accept however I do it. A single toss.'

She flipped. The coin spun poorly and fell to the carpet.

'Tails,' called Cathy gleefully.

'Me then,' said Ellie reluctantly. 'What am I going to wear?'

'I've got some shorts, a bit baggy for you, but they'll do,' said Vicky, 'a T-shirt too.'

'You'll need a plank or something to brush out the marks,' said Cathy, 'a bucket if the mud has hardened... In fact, I'd best come with you.'

'Why?' said Ellie.

'I don't want you doing it badly.'

Ten minutes later, both of them in ill-fitting shorts, t-shirts, flip-flops, and with various bits of gear in the wheelbarrow headed down to the lake.

Chapter 20

Jack drew into the car park at the front of the school building. There were three other cars there. The Head's in his marked parking place. One of the others he knew as Ellie's, while the third had its four doors wide open and a pair of legs in tracksuit bottoms poking out of the back seat. A bucket and a bowl of water lay nearby. Someone was obviously having a good clean out.

'What do you think?' said Jack once he'd locked up.

They were looking at the red brick building, the high windows and gothic ornamentation about the eaves and windows, and at the pillared portico. Victorian classical, built to impress.

'It's alright,' said Mia with a shrug, refusing to be impressed.

The person in the car came out on hearing their voices. It was a woman in ill-fitting clothing, in her hands a large sponge. Over her hair she had a shower cap and was wearing yellow plastic gloves.

'Good morning,' called Jack.

The woman frowned. 'Good morning,' she said. And returned to her work, ducking back into the back seat of the car.

Ellie's sister, thought Jack. Even in her oversized clothing he could see they were remarkably alike. On another occasion he might have easily mistaken her. Though she had rather dressed down for the occasion.

He'd left some of his tools in the classroom and brought out another toolbox with extras. He had a last think what he might need. It was a nuisance to keep going backwards and forwards just for a screwdriver or chisel. Satisfied, they climbed the steps to the main door and went in a small side door to which the caretaker had given Jack the door code.

They came into the marble floored vestibule. Directly in front was a wide curving staircase. To the side a glass cabinet full of silver cups and plaques. At head height around the walls were a series of wide school photos. They each had the same composition. The youngest students sat on the grass, then a rank of students sitting on chairs, behind them older students standing, and finally, presumably standing on benches, a row of the oldest students. The photos began in black and white and in the 70s colour began. On one side, above the photos, was a large portrait in a gilded frame of the current headmaster in a mortar board and holding a scroll. Directly opposite was one of his father, similarly attired.

Their footsteps echoed in the corridor.

'Where is everyone?' whispered Mia.

'On holiday,' said Jack. 'Some teachers might be in later.'

'How come they trust you here on your own?'

Jack laughed. 'You have to trust a builder.'

'You could be a crook,' she said.

'You can't go about not trusting everyone,' he said. 'Otherwise nothing would get done. Cleaners have to come in too, plumbers. Besides, anything valuable is behind locked doors.'

'Spose so.'

They'd come to the classroom where he was working, the door open. Some of his tools lay on a dirty sheet on a table. He took his toolbox in. Mia followed.

'I'm working here,' he said. 'So this is where you'll find me.'

Mia went to the window.

'This is where the burglars broke in,' she said. 'Then smashed the classroom door to get out...' She followed the crooks' trail into the corridor. 'Then broke that door to the computer room.'

'It all makes work for the working man,' he said.

'Why weren't the burglar alarms on?'

Jack laughed. 'You should be in the police force.'

They went down the corridor to the library. Ellie had said she'd open it for him. Had she remembered? She had.

They went in. It was as large as a medium hall with bookshelves round most of the sides, and aisles of them running parallel. Here and there were tables with computers.

'All yours,' he said.

'It's massive,' she said.

'There might be one or two books you haven't read in here,' he said.

'DVDs, all along there,' she said, and turned a computer on. It rapidly sprang into life.

'I'll leave you,' he said. 'You know where I am. We'll have tea at 10 o'clock.'

He left, a little worried at leaving her on her own. But there were loads of books and movies. He was concerned about a whole day of this for her. Could he finish today? Not if he had to entertain her. He'd need at least tomorrow morning then. And you never knew with building work. Something you didn't expect came up, or a part you didn't have.

Jack returned to the classroom. He had to put the lock in. He took the new one out of its plastic. And began measuring and marking up the door where it would go.

Chapter 21

Jenny was emptying drawers on the bed, packing the clothing into plastic bags. She'd already done the bookshelves, there was the wardrobe still to do, the under-bed drawers, and all the toys left about which she'd distinctly said tidy up before you go to Nan's. Though more in hope than expectation.

Ten days she'd had of this. She was utterly sick of it. Destroying the life they'd had here. This morning she'd begun work in tears. Another room to be stripped clean. The place they were going to only had two bedrooms. It was poky, the wallpaper horrible. The kitchen too small, the garden a pocket handkerchief and a dirty one at that. A stopgap, she hoped. But then they had to find work... She could see nothing bright ahead.

It was like digging your own grave before they shot you. There were no benefits. As if it were a punishment for a sin known only to a god who didn't respond to mortals, simply scourged them.

She emptied the last drawers from the chest of drawers. Some of the socks were hardly worth keeping. She threw a torn vest on the floor.

George came in with two cups of tea. He handed her one and sank onto the bed with his own.

'You haven't done anything this morning,' she said, 'and you look shattered already.'

'I can hardly put one leg in front of the other,' he said.

'You were tossing and turning all night.'

'Couldn't sleep.'

She sighed. 'This does get you down. But there's no help for it, George. We've got to do it. And you can't leave it all to me.'

'Leave it,' he said, a hand on her arm.

She looked at him as if he had sworn at her. 'What?'

'I said leave it.' He held her arm more tightly.

'The house has to be ready when the furniture van comes on Saturday,' she said. 'Let go of my arm.'

'He's dead,' he said.

'George, what are you talking about?'

'Mr DeNeuve is dead.'

Suddenly she was alert, looking around the room, thinking of everything they had done, thinking there was a spark of a chance...

'How do you know?' she said.

If he'd been less tired he might not have begun, but the first words had been said and he had to tell her that things had changed for them. And he told her about last night and his encounter at the lake while he was walking the dog.

'I said give me the house back and our jobs – and I haven't seen anything.'

'They killed him? Mrs DeNeuve, Cathy and Ellie?' she queried, eyes wide.

'His missus and two daughters. Yep. Threw him blind drunk in the lake.'

'Is he there now?'

'I haven't looked,' he said, 'but I can't see how he wouldn't be.'

'It's murder,' she said. 'And you're implicated.'

'You said you hated the old fart.'

'I didn't say kill him.'

'I didn't kill him.'

'But you didn't save him.' She put a hand over his. 'And you know who did kill him.'

'So do you.'

They were silent a while. Neither drank their tea. Jenny looked about the room, at the plastic bags filled, at the toys, at the wardrobe, shut and forbidding. She imagined the lake, the coots and swans, and something floating... No – not the lake. She would not see that.

'And Mrs DeNeuve really said we've got the house back?' she said.

'She did.'

'All this...' she began, swinging her arm round to indicate the room and contents, 'can stop?'

'This is our house, Jenny. We live here again.'

Her hands slapped to her cheeks. 'My God, my God – I cannot believe we can stop packing.'

Suddenly she was weeping. He pulled her to him and held her.

'No more packing, love. But no unpacking for a while. We don't know he's dead. Get it? So if anyone comes, we are taking a break. That's all.'

'I don't know what to do,' she said. All her attention had been on packing. On the move. And now there was no move. She wiped her eyes with her sleeve.

'I'll hoe the garden,' she said. 'Then give it a good water.'

'Isn't that a bit suspicious?' he said.

She smiled at him. 'No, no, George. It's what gardeners do. You leave the garden in good shape for whoever moves in.'

Chapter 22

Ellie left the school house with her laptop. She'd had another shower, shampooed again, the works, as if to wash last night completely away. Her clothes were freshly clean. Her and Cathy's shorts, t-shirts and flip-flops from their work at the lakeside were whirring in the faithful washing machine. Mother was along the garden path searching out any drippings.

It was a lovely day. The sky a squinting blue, a few fluffy clouds left behind. She looked ahead, purposely not directing her gaze at the lake as she strolled along the path to the school. Not that she would likely have seen the corpse through the trees, but you never knew, things float on water. What was done, was now utterly done, but you don't have to look and check. It wasn't a dream. But it yet had to be revealed to people at large.

This was limbo, the patch of time when they must pretend all is right with the world, and go on as if nothing untoward has happened. Until someone, none of the family of course, found the body and they could react suitably. Her current task was to prime the someone. If it wasn't to be family or the caretaker, then all that was left was the builder. An innocent party. She would subtly persuade him to go down to the lake.

In the car park, Cathy was cleaning the inside of her car. When Ellie came through, she was wringing out a sponge, wearing an ancient tracksuit of their mother's.

'This is the fourth change of water,' she said. 'Can you smell anything?'

Ellie poked her head in the rear of the car and sniffed. She could smell detergent fragrance and that was all. She put her head down the gully between the front and back seats. No smell of shit, vomit or urine. No detritus of the human body.

'Immaculate,' she said.

Cathy was holding a hand vacuum cleaner. 'I'll give it a last going over. And then that's that.' She pressed her lips. 'Your builder's in. And brought a little girl with him.'

'His daughter.'

'What right has he...' she began.

'I gave him permission,' interrupted Ellie.

'You would. Of course,' said Cathy. 'Him, being your builder.'

'I am going to casually suggest he might go down to the lake for his tea break...'

'Don't make it too obvious,' said Cathy.

'I'm not totally incompetent.'

Cathy smiled. And Ellie knew she was thinking of their clean up last night by the lake. She wouldn't admit it to Cathy, but was grateful to have her sister there. Scraping the surface with the board, removing the tyre marks and their footprints, wetting the surface with the bucket where it had hardened... Cathy had been organised. She more scatty, not being able to help herself looking at the just visible thing floating so close to the shore. Getting back to her mother's she hadn't slept much, and was surviving now on adrenaline, caffeine and nerves. All would catch up with her. This limbo would break into pieces. The world would know.

Cathy was vacuuming again. Such a thorough clean up they had done. Could there possibly be a single hair they'd missed?

'See you at lunch,' Ellie said, and headed for the school entrance.

Chapter 23

Jack was chiselling into the doorjamb, a large chisel to get on the move. It wouldn't matter if it was rough and ready as it would be covered by the plate. But he liked to do a decent job if he could, though it was amazing what you could cover up. What lay under a smooth surface layer.

He put down the rubber mallet and wondered whether he should go and see Mia in the library. Then thought no, finish this. The aim was to be done today. Half an hour say, then go and see her for a tea break. Or maybe take her over to the caretaker's.

He felt guilty at bringing her in. But the whole thing had been sprung on him.

He switched to a quarter inch chisel to work on the corners. Gentle taps. Sharp tools.

And heard a car pull into the car park. Curious, he went to the window. It was the caretaker in his van, and he saw, at once, the back was stuffed with computers. They had to be those from the boathouse. The stolen ones. What was going on?

He noted he was not the only one watching. Cathy had stopped her clean up and was standing arms akimbo as George got out. He said something to her, she said something angrily back. He flapped an arm and went back to his van. She shouted something which he ignored as he took out a trolley and began loading computers onto it. Cathy remained eyeballing him as if she was willing a curse.

It was then Ellie came into the classroom.

'Good morning, Jack,' she said. 'How's it going?'

'Look at this,' he said.

She came to the window. And her face darkened.

'He's taken them out of the boathouse,' he said. 'In plain sight. I don't get it.'

'It's some insurance fiddle,' said Ellie dismissively. 'Forget it.'

The caretaker's trolley now full, he leaned it back and wheeled it to the ramp at the front entrance, then up its slope and through the school door, observed by the three of them. Even when he'd disappeared, Cathy remained watching the door he'd gone through, as if she might by her fluence pull him back.

'Aren't you supposed to do such things in secret?' he said shaking his head. He turned to Ellie. 'You don't know anything about this scam, do you?'

'No.'

The way she turned away, he wondered whether she did.

'All this breaking of doors and windows...' he said. 'It's such a charade.'

She came to him. 'If he hadn't, you wouldn't be here.'

He ran a finger round her eye.

'You didn't sleep well last night.'

'Hardly at all,' she said. 'Worry. The school. Family stuff. You know.'

'How's your dad this morning? Quite a headache, I should think.'

'I haven't seen him,' she said with a shrug. 'He must've got up early.'

'I didn't see him in his office.'

'He'll be somewhere about the school,' she said, and then indicated the open window. 'It's a lovely day. Too lovely to be cooped up in here. You should have your tea break by the lake...'

'I think I will. I'll take my daughter down.'

'Oh, I'd forgotten about her.'

'She's in the library. Watching a movie last time I looked in. Some Harry Potter thing.'

A sound from the window drew him back. George was returning with the trolley, presumably for another load. Cathy was patently ignoring him and had gone back to her cleaning.

'I always try to keep in with caretakers,' he said as he watched George taking a computer out of his car. 'They can make life difficult for you. But George... It's more than that. He seems to be able to do what he wants here.' Then he reflected. 'Except he's been sacked, he's moving out. This doesn't make sense... It's as if he's daring you.'

'Does it really matter?' said Ellie. 'Besides, I came to see you. You've got sawdust in your hair.' She brushed some out, fuzzing his hair.

He kissed her. She threw her arms about him and embraced him back, gluing their mouths and bodies, hands seeking places.

'You are preventing a workman in the course of his trade,' he murmured.

'Profit and loss,' she moaned.

Chapter 24

Mia had seen this movie three times anyway. It wasn't a lot of fun on your own. No one to say 'this is a good bit' to, to laugh at with. Earlier she'd looked at the science section in the library and was scathing at the astronomy books. Though it was possible the good ones were out. That's what happens. The rubbish gets left behind. She half read a novel, played a computer game. Too educational. They never had the really good ones in schools. And then fixed on a movie... But all this space, on her own. She could have smashed everything up, if she'd a mind.

She felt a bit ashamed. All these books, games, and movies, and she was bored. Like a little kid. But what she wanted was company. She'd go and see her dad. Persuade him to go outside for a while.

She turned off the computer. She had her backpack with a few edibles in, but Dad had the tea and chocolate biscuits. She went out into the corridor, closing the door behind her. The corridor stretched on like a hospital to a final door, way down. It was ghostly. All the emptiness, the high ceiling. No one in sight. Anything could come along this passage. She would run and scream and the sound would be lost in the volume. She shivered. She wanted her dad.

She could phone Mum. It would probably be OK, unless she was having some operation, having her breasts cut off or something just as painful.

That was her Dad's classroom. He wasn't at the door working. There he was, back by the shelving, kissing a woman. Heavens, they were going at it. Mia pulled back, so she was almost hidden by the door. He'd said he didn't have a girlfriend, though he certainly seemed to have one now.

She felt uncomfortable watching. It wasn't like in a film. It was your dad and some woman. And all so animal and noisy.

The couple released each other. The woman stroked his face, he was looking into her eyes. Then she opened a door behind them, a stock cupboard or something. And the two of them went in.

And Mia knew what for! And she wasn't going to stay. Fancy! In a stock cupboard. Her dad. And was she a teacher? None of her teachers would do anything like that. Maybe independent schools were different.

She marched fiercely down the hallway, wanting to get away. Were they taking their clothes off? Stop it, stop it. She mustn't think about such things. In a stock cupboard!

Once out in the open air, she felt better. The sun was warm in a brilliant sky, a slight breeze blowing. Sex in theory was alright. She knew all about it. Well, quite a bit about it. But it's not the same when it's your mum and dad. Her mum had had a couple of boyfriends and Mia had heard them in the bedroom at night. Then in the morning she was just the same as she ever was, as if she hadn't had all those things done to her, and maybe done all sorts of things herself... But her dad wasn't like that.

Oh yes, he was. They were practically eating each other. And in the stock cupboard, going at it like goats.

Yuk!

She had drifted down to the trees. How long did sex take, before she could go back and pretend she hadn't seen anything? Quarter of an hour maybe. He'd said he'd be over for their tea break. She wasn't sure she wanted him to be. Not after where he'd been.

There was the lake, down there, sunlight twinkling on its fractured surface. A family of ducks glided by the island. There was something there, floating by the shore.

It looked like a man.

Chapter 25

Jack's phone rang.

He sat up and looked at his phone, the only thing lit up in the darkness.

'It's my daughter,' he exclaimed. 'I'd better answer it.'

Ellie was rising, creaking, half moaning. He could smell sweat and cooped up sex.

'Hello, Mia,' he said as lightly as he could. 'You OK?'

'Dad, there's a dead man in the lake.'

'You sure?'

'Course I am. I'm by the lake. He's just there, two metres away. Please come, right away.'

'Be there in two minutes, love. Don't panic, I'll be there.'

He switched off almost the same instant as the stock room light came on.

'What's going on?' Ellie said.

Ellie wore only a t-shirt and socks, scattered about lay her knickers, bra and jeans.

'She says there's someone dead in the lake.'

'You'd better go at once.'

He kissed her on the cheek, and pulled his jeans on. His pants he shoved in his pocket. The same with his socks as he slipped into his trainers.

And was out the door, running.

It was only then he wondered why Ellie wasn't coming. It was her school, her lake. But then it was his daughter. Halfway down the corridor, he tripped over a shoelace. He stopped and tucked them in the sides of his trainers and ran on. Along the long hallway, all at once grown up again. Screwing in stock room cupboards was for teenagers.

Into the vestibule, and across the space where arrays of schoolchildren smiled perpetually in the sunlight. Out the door and into the car park. The caretaker was gone, Cathy's car was locked up.

Across and into the copse of trees and down the hill, where he could make out Mia standing by the lake, looking up towards him. Responsible parent coming in fast. She spread her arms and waved.

'Dad! Dad!'

'Coming, Mia!'

There was something behind her. In the lake, gaining in human form as he rapidly homed in.

And then he was there, breathless. And his daughter rushed to him and threw her arms round him.

'It's a dead man, Dad.'

He held her to him as he walked the few paces to the water's edge. And there, face down in the water, a man in a suit, the jacket fanned out as if he was trying to fly. What he could see of the face was white like fish flesh. He knew him; the man he had wheel-barrowed home yesterday.

And almost certainly dead. Face down, how could he be alive? But just in case, Jack slipped off his trainers and waded into the water. It was cold about his ankles. The body was only a pace or two off the shore. He bent low and flipped the corpse over, splashing himself as the arms flapped.

The eyes were closed, the skin on his face white and bubbly. There was a snail on his cheek. There could be no doubt the headmaster was well and truly dead.

Jack came out of the water where Mia was watching.

'Is he dead, Dad?'

'Yes, he is. And I'd better phone the police. I'm sure it's some sort of accident.'

He took out his phone. Was it 999, or some other number as this was no emergency? But he didn't know the other number. 999 would have to do. He dialled.

'Which service do you require?'

He wasn't sure of this. But it was too late for an ambulance.

'Give me the police.'

Chapter 26

Jack put his arm round Mia's shoulder and led her away from the lake. He needed to tell people, the caretaker and of course, the DeNeuves. He didn't know how long the police would be. Five minutes? An hour? They walked up the hill, into the cool of the trees. He felt guilty at having left her this morning, especially doing what he was doing. But then he wasn't to know there was a body in the lake. And Mia was a sensible kid, so normally nothing would have happened.

Except he was responsible. He should have been keeping an eye on her. She must have come past the classroom when she was going out. And any other time he'd have seen her. Could even be she'd come to see him but he'd not been visible. He wouldn't enquire, as she might ask him where he was. And he'd prefer not to lie. He wondered what Ellie was doing. It already seemed ages ago when they'd been going at it on the floor of the stock room. Twenty minutes ago, maybe.

Then he saw her. She was striding towards the big house. She was a little way ahead, on the higher road and walking faster, so she couldn't see him. Well, he'd catch up with her later.

'How did the man die?' said Mia.

'Well, you can't be sure,' he said. 'They'll have to investigate, but I know he drank a lot, so I'd guess he got very drunk and collapsed in the lake. And drowned.'

'You used to get drunk,' she said. 'I remember.'

That hurt. It wasn't a good thing to be remembered for. The state he'd been in.

'I was pretty stupid,' he said. 'You'd be surprised how many grown ups are. They pour the stuff down...'

102

'It tastes horrible,' she said.

'You get used to it.'

'I don't want to get used to it.'

'Very sensible,' he said.

'But why get drunk anyway? It makes you an idiot, it makes you sick. It makes you fall in the lake and die.'

'It's quite nice to start with,' he said. 'Drink makes you happy, and that's where you should stop. But lots of people can't. I couldn't.'

'Why, Dad?'

'I wasn't happy. In fact I was miserable. And when you get drunk, you don't know or feel anything anymore. You're a staggering lump of nothing.'

'I'd rather be miserable,' she said.

He tugged at her shoulder. 'And so would I.'

They had reached the gatehouse. They went through the front garden gate and up the path to the front door which was wide open.

'Hello!' called Jack into the hallway which seemed a little emptier than on his last visit.

George came out of a side room.

'Hello, Jack. Come in.'

'This is my daughter, Mia. I can't stay. I've just got some news for you.'

Jenny came running down the stairs.

'Do you want a cup of tea, Jack? This your daughter?'

'Yes, this is Mia.'

'Hello,' she said shyly.

'Come in, come in,' said Jenny eagerly. 'I'll put the kettle on.'

'I can't stay,' he said. 'And I've got news...'

'What news?' said George.

'There's no easy way to say this,' he began. 'But Mia went down to the lake a little while ago...'

'And I found a drowned man,' she said.

Jenny's hands went to her mouth. 'Oh no!'

'Who?' said George.

'The headmaster,' said Jack.

George and Jenny looked at each other.

'You sure?' said George.

'I am,' said Jack. 'And I've phoned the police.'

'He was lying face down in the water,' said Mia. 'His face was all white and crinkly, he had a snail on one cheek...'

'Oh, how terrible for you!' said Jenny.

'Quite a shock, I'm sure,' said George.

'My advice is don't go down there,' said Jack. 'The police will be here soon. And they'll have to investigate. You know what cops are like. Ask questions. It's obvious what happened but they have to make sure.'

'Of course,' said Jenny. 'He fell in drunk. I knew it was going to happen one day. I've seen him in the school, absolutely blotto. Staggering down the hallway.'

They were silent for a little while, taking in the new knowledge.

'Might change things for you,' said Jack. 'The owner dead. His wife might have a different view on your position.'

'Good point, Jack,' said George. 'Do they know yet?'

'It's my next port of call, to tell them.'

Jenny turned to her husband. She said, 'Do you think, George? Mrs DeNeuve might reconsider...'

'I get on better with her,' said her husband. 'She might very well see things differently. Seventeen years' service. I've worked hard here.'

'Oh George! Do you think it's possible we can stay?'

'Don't count your horses yet, love. But you never know... Don't do any more packing until I've had a chat with Mrs DeNeuve.'

'And I'd best be off there. Not that I'm looking forward to it,' said Jack.

'Be quite a shock, I'm sure,' said Jenny.

'Can you look after Mia?' said Jack, 'While I go over. I won't be very long.'

'Of course, of course. Come in, dear,' said Jenny. 'You've had a terrible shock. Come and have some tea and cake. Or maybe you'd prefer a coke?'

'Won't be long,' called Jack.

And he left them.

He had an uneasy feeling as he made his way to the big house. The way the caretaker and his wife looked at each other, their enthusiasm. It was as if George and Jenny had known already, and had been acting up for him.

Chapter 27

Jack was in the sitting room with the three DeNeuves. Not an easy experience. He was standing, Vicky was in an armchair, Cathy on the sofa and Ellie seated on the arm of the other armchair. She caught his eye and looked away guiltily. Cathy had taken off the baggy tracksuit, obviously not her own, and was back in her dress suit.

'You say your daughter found him, Mr Bell?' said Vicky.

'Yes, she did.'

'She shouldn't have been here at all,' said Cathy.

'I said he could bring her in,' said Ellie.

'Well you shouldn't have done. Employees can't bring their children in whenever they feel like it.'

'Her mother had to go into hospital for an operation,' Jack intervened, unsure about the operation but deciding exaggeration was his best ploy.

'I still don't think...' said Cathy.

'We'll allow it this time, Mr Bell,' said Vicky.

'He did bring Daddy back yesterday,' said Ellie.

'Fat lot of good that did him,' said Cathy.

Jack thought, let's get out of here, now that I have told them. He felt like a child, getting a telling off, as if he was somehow responsible for Mr DeNeuve's death. Ellie had told him her sister was a cow, which he now thought unfair on cattle. And her mother thought she was the Queen.

'I've phoned the police,' said Jack.

'Should you have done?' queried Cathy. 'Isn't that our prerogative?'

He stiffened, wanting to tell where to go, but quelled the desire. He still had a job here and might as well keep it.

'I found a dead man in the lake, Miss DeNeuve. And that's the law. I am very sorry it's your husband, Mrs DeNeuve. But the police have to be called. And the sooner the better.'

'That's common sense, Mummy,' said Ellie.

'He should inform his employer first,' said Cathy to her mother. 'That is the correct way of doing things. There are proper ways.' She stared at Jack. 'This is our school, Mr Bell. And you must come through us. You work here with our permission. Is that clear?'

He held her look, not about to be cowed. This was a tiddly job. Two to three days at most. It had already caused him enough trouble. The worst they could do was sack him.

'It's clear,' he said. 'And I'll do the work as laid down. If it requires changes I'll ask you first. But this wasn't about work. It's about a body in the lake.' He shook his head. 'And as we are not going to agree, I suggest we ask the police whether I did the right thing or not.'

'Has ownership no rights, Mr Bell?' said Cathy.

'Ask the police, Miss DeNeuve.' He turned to Vicky. 'Please accept my sympathy, Mrs DeNeuve. I am sorry to be the bearer of such sad news. I only did what I thought was the best in the circumstances.'

'Thank you, Mr Bell,' said Vicky. 'I appreciate your condolences. And I am sorry your daughter had to be the one to find my husband.'

'She shouldn't have been there in the first place,' exclaimed Cathy.

'Thank you, Mr Bell,' said Ellie, ignoring her sister. 'We appreciate you taking the trouble.'

The doorbell rang.

Ellie ran out.

'Unless there's anything else, I'll be off, ladies,' said Jack. He all but had to stop himself from bowing and backing out. He turned to Cathy. 'And I'll be taking my daughter away once the police have come.'

He turned to leave as Ellie returned.

'The police are here,' said Ellie. 'And they want to see Mr Bell.'

PART THREE:
WORKING IT ALL OUT

Chapter 28

Jack was standing where he'd been ordered, while the two plain clothes police officers looked at the body. They had driven down from the gatehouse with Jack on board. At the lake, once Jack had pointed out the body they'd put on plastic overshoes and gloves, and told Jack to stay back. The officers went to the lakeside and gingerly stepped into the water to examine the body, touching it as little as possible.

He was perhaps ten metres away watching them, looking at the footprints in the mud by the side of the lake. The only ones he could make out were his and Mia's, though with some prints overstepping others it was confusing in places.

The police officers left the corpse and came back to him. The senior was Detective Inspector Sarah Jones, a severe woman in her mid 40s, wearing a navy blue skirt and jacket, with a white shirt open at the collar, blonde hair tied back. Her colleague was a black man, perhaps ten years younger in a bluish grey suit.

She said to her colleague, 'We'd best make this a crime scene, Zak. Can you contact SOCO?'

Jack was surprised. 'You think this was a crime?'

She turned to him. 'I don't know, sir. But I've learnt it pays to keep an open mind. Don't assume one way or another at the outset.'

'He was very drunk yesterday,' said Jack.

'So you were saying in the car,' said the Inspector. 'You ferried him back home in a wheelbarrow?'

Her colleague had wandered off and was on the phone.

'Totally unconscious,' said Jack. 'I found him in the school corridor...'

'And the next time you saw him was here?'

'Yes. My daughter found him. And she called me.'

'Your daughter? What was she doing here, Mr Bell?'

'Her mother has gone into hospital. I was stuck with what to do with her. She's eleven. And Ellie DeNeuve said I could bring her in. She was in the library this morning, got bored and went for a wander...'

'Can I see the bottom of your boots?'

Jack was surprised at the change of tack, but did as he was bid, and stood on one leg and turned a boot over.

'Thank you,' said Inspector Jones, looking closely at the sole and then at the footprints in the mud. 'We'll need to eliminate you and your daughter's prints. We'll photograph them. And see what others there may be here.'

'Will that be long?' said Jack. He wanted to take Mia away, guilty at his neglect of her, at the fact she'd left the school to explore, no doubt, because she couldn't find him.

'Soonish,' she said, looking at her watch. 'Did you know Mr DeNeuve?'

'I've only been here since yesterday,' he said. 'They had a break-in, and I'm repairing a window and a couple of doors. I saw Mr DeNeuve about. Ferried him home drunk yesterday, but we never spoke. I get the feeling he's a bit of a snob. Doesn't talk to workmen.'

'Well, I suppose it goes with this sort of place,' she said. 'Local comprehensive myself. We'll need to have a quick word with your daughter. You can be present. Don't worry, nothing heavy. And one more thing: did you move the body?'

'I turned him over. He was face down in the water. I wasn't totally sure he was dead, so I thought best make sure, to see if I could do anything.'

'Perfectly understandable, Mr Bell. That'll do for now... Where will you be?'

'I'm going up to the gatehouse where my daughter is. The caretaker and his wife are keeping an eye on her. I want to leave as soon as possible... I'm not sure how she's coping.'

'I'll get you and your daughter dealt with as soon as possible, Mr Bell. Please tell the caretaker and whoever lives with him not to come down here. It's a crime scene now. And we don't want it contaminated. Thank you, Mr Bell.'

Having dismissed Jack, she went off to talk to her colleague. Jack was relieved; she'd been polite enough but he was never comfortable talking to the police, not being sure they weren't judging him for use later. And they might yet be heavy on him about Mia coming down to the lake on her own. He was sure Ellie would stay mum about their love making, and hoped Mia would leave out unnecessary details. Not that that he and Ellie had committed any crime, but it might give the cops a laugh at his expense.

Halfway to the gatehouse, well away from the police, he made a phone call. One he'd been avoiding for months. The phone rang and he waited nervously, half hoping it wouldn't be answered.

'Hello,' came a familiar voice.

'Hello, Mum.'

'Is that you, Jack?'

'It is, Mum. How are you?'

'Fine mostly. A bit of rheumatism. I had a cataract operation last month. But mustn't grumble. You OK?'

'On the wagon,' he said, 'for eighteen months now. I've been meaning to phone, but keep putting it off. Taking that money, you know.'

'It did leave me short,' she said, 'but that's history. Forget it.'

'Well, I am sorry. Believe me. You at home?'

'I am. Retired now. Your dad's left. More history for you. He ran off with a woman at work. I don't know where he is. And I can't say I care much. How's Mia and Alison?'

'I'm divorced,' he said. 'I was a wreck, as you know, and Alison decided enough was enough. Mia is with me today. I wondered if you'd like to see her?'

'I'd love to.'

'There's a bit of a scene here at work. Can I bring her over?'

'Of course you can, Jack. Lots to catch up on. And I do want to see my granddaughter... I bet she'll be as tall as me now.'

'Not sure exactly when I can get away. There's a few things to sort out here. An hour or two. I'll phone before I leave.'

'That'll give me time to do some shopping.'

They said their goodbyes and rang off.

Jack leaned against a tree. He'd done it. They hadn't said much, but it was surprisingly exhausting. Mia would be his buffer when he got there.

He continued to the gatehouse.

Chapter 29

He joined Mia on the lawn in the gatehouse garden, having told Jenny and George he needed to have a word with her. She was making a daisy chain. He joined in but soon gave up. His heart wasn't in it, and she'd catch him out for trying too hard. Even as a kid, daisy chains seemed a waste of flowers. In no time, they curled up and died.

'You OK, love?'

'I think so.' She was concentrating on her daisy chain, threading a stalk of one into a hole she'd made in the last stalk in the chain.

'You won't have nightmares?'

Even as he said it, it sounded a silly question. Which only wanted one answer.

'I don't know,' she said.

He put a hand on her arm.

'I'm sorry you had to find him.'

She wouldn't look at him, and took his hand away. He needed to find out exactly where they were at. Wanted to tell her – don't tell your mother, but felt he wasn't anywhere near the point where he could.

She said, 'I went to find you in the classroom.' Mia looked up from her daisy chain, her face stern. 'And saw you kissing a lady. And then you went into a cupboard with her.'

Hell. She knew. Or maybe she didn't. She was only eleven. He couldn't imagine what she might think.

Out of the blue, he said, 'She was going to show me something.'

'What?'

'Some pictures.'

'What of?'

'Horses.'

'Why?'

'There's a boy in her class who's a really good drawer...'

'And not to do anything else?' She stared at him, her face screwed up in examination. God, she reminded him of Alison. That accusatory face.

'Just to look at pictures,' he said. 'He was really good, the boy.'

'You can show them to me later,' she said. She had a slight smile. Of disbelief, he thought. But at least he had other plans for her. And she might forget the pictures. But later was later, it was dealing with now that mattered.

'I phoned my mother, your Nan,' he said. 'I said I'd take you over when the police have finished with us.'

'I haven't seen her for ages,' she said. 'She was always nice.'

To you, thought Jack. Occasional visits with treats. But anyway, he thought children should see their grannies. And sons shouldn't take from their mother's purse.

'She really wants to see you,' he said.

'I'd like to see her,' she said.

And was deep in her daisy chain once more, digging her nail into a stem and threading a fresh one through. It was good, he thought. It was calming. She seemed perfectly alright. But what a bundle of lies he'd told her! They might yet rebound on him. Too late. He had made up a tale on the hoof about their time in the cupboard. But how could he have told her the truth?

'I want to have a word with Jenny and George,' he said. 'Do you mind?'

'No.'

Head down, the daisy chain in her lap perhaps a metre long, she looked so small. A child. Yet she'd seen a dead body, but what could he say to her? That she hadn't seen a body? That bodies didn't matter? In the midst of life we are in death – or something. That bombs are falling every day, Kalashnikovs spitting bullets in war zones. That we all die one way or another?

What do you say to a child?

Alison would know. But she was in hospital. And was the last person he'd ask.

George and Jenny were at the ironwork table on the patio. They were waiting for him when he came to join them. He'd noted their impatience when he was talking to Mia, wanting to pump him. Jenny poured him a cup of tea. A prelude. He wasn't sure he wanted to speak to them, but he didn't want to sit silent and stupid with Mia.

'What's happening down there, Jack?' said George.

'It's a crime scene,' he said. 'They don't want anyone going there.'

'A crime scene!' declared Jenny. 'How can that be?'

'The Detective Inspector said she is keeping an open mind.'

'But you told them you took him home drunk? Didn't you?' said George.

'I did.'

'Stupid plods,' said Jenny vehemently. 'The man drank like a fish. I always said he'd end up in the lake one day. Didn't I, George?'

'You did.'

'Why do they want to make a murder out of an obvious accident?' she exclaimed. 'Why?'

'Did they find anything, apart from the body?' said George.

'No,' said Jack. 'I don't think so, anyway. They had a quick look at the body, asked me a few questions and decided they'd best declare it a crime scene. No one is to go down there.'

'Before we know it, there'll be the papers here,' said Jenny, throwing her hands up. 'Why can't they see the obvious?'

Because they've got a job to do, thought Jack. And sometimes the obvious isn't what happened. He didn't say it, not wanting to enter into an argument. Everyone was on edge anyway.

'They like to make everyone nervous,' said George. 'Show their power.'

'A drunken man falls in the water. Open and shut case,' said Jenny. 'Don't you think so, Jack?'

Put on the spot, he had to say something. 'It's possible,' he began, 'that someone might have taken advantage of the fact that he was drunk.'

'Who?' retorted Jenny.

'I don't know.'

'You think them DeNeuves?'

'I'm just saying,' he said uncomfortably, 'that's it's possible. Maybe that's what the cops are thinking.'

'You've got an evil mind, Jack.'

'No, be fair, Jenny,' said George. 'He's only saying what he thinks the cops are thinking.'

Jenny ignored her husband. 'You saw him absolutely paralytic. Carted him off home in a wheelbarrow, for heaven's sake. Out to the world. A drunken slob. It's obvious what happens next. He begins to wake up, finds another bottle and goes staggering away drinking it...'

'Where's the bottle?' said Jack.

'What?'

'You said he went staggering away drinking.'

'I don't know. I wasn't there.'

'And that's why it's a crime scene,' he said. 'Neither were they.'

They were all silent. Jack wished he hadn't started on the subject. He distrusted this couple. They were hiding something. Mia though was patiently making her garland. The most sensible of us, he thought.

'You've stopped packing,' he said. Maybe unpacking, he thought.

George caught Jenny's eye. 'We don't know what to do,' he said. 'He was the one gave us notice. Now he's dead, his wife might decide different.'

'But it's not the right time to talk to her,' said Jenny.

'So we're going to leave things a few hours,' said George. 'I'll maybe go over this evening and talk to them.'

'Yes. You've only got a few days,' said Jack, trying to be sympathetic.

'I've a feeling she'll be on our side,' said George. 'It was him wanted us out.'

The Detective Sergeant came out into the garden with a man who, obvious from the large camera hanging from his neck, was the photographer.

'Hello, everyone. I'm Detective Sergeant Wilson. As I'm sure you all know by now, there's been a body found in the lake and we will need to question you all. If we might begin with your daughter, Mr Bell. You can accompany her.'

Chapter 30

Vicky was in her customary armchair. She had a handkerchief in the lap of a dark blue, long dress. Not yet ready for black. Although she knew he was dead, she wasn't to be seen as knowing too soon. The knowledge had to be taken in precise steps. Jack had informed her only half an hour before. She must be numb, lifeless, disbelieving.

Detective Inspector Jones was seated on the sofa, a notebook and pen in her lap.

'Your daughters have identified the body, Mrs DeNeuve. There is no doubt it's your husband. Please accept my sympathy.'

Vicky dabbed her eyes. 'Thank you, Inspector. I cannot believe this. I am overwhelmed. I was up this morning, preparing to do some work on my garden – and then out of nowhere... this!' She shook her head. 'We never know what's in store. I cannot believe it.'

'I know it's very soon, Mrs DeNeuve, but can you manage a few questions?'

'I think so.'

She mustn't overdo it. Nor underdo it. She was the caring wife, trying to be strong for the family. This was so important, their initial judgement. She must be distraught. But trying in spite of it. And she must lead them to the place where she wanted them to be.

'When did you last see your husband, Mrs DeNeuve?'

'About ten o'clock last night, on that sofa, Inspector.' She sniffed and wiped her eyes. 'He'd passed out, drunk. All very shameful really. The builder, Mr Bell, brought him back on a wheelbarrow. I went to bed about ten. He was still unconscious laid out on the sofa where you are sitting.'

'Weren't you worried about him?'

'I've seen him like that before,' she said. 'He'd wake up in his own time.'

'But he wasn't there this morning, was he?'

'No,' said Vicky. 'I assumed he'd gone to the school.'

'Even with a massive hangover?' queried DI Jones.

'Especially with a massive hangover,' she said. 'Ashamed of himself. He'd rather suffer alone in his office. Pretend to us he's working. A game we played. Middle class pride you might say. He could make out he hadn't got drunk, and I'd not mention it. I was going to call him at lunchtime, see if he wanted any food... Not very likely, but part of the game.'

'So he got drunk quite often, Mrs DeNeuve.'

'Too often.'

'Why?'

'Stress,' she said with a sigh. 'The school has financial problems but we are sorting them out. A new school year is about to begin. And habit. His drug of choice.' She wiped her eyes. 'This is so distressing. I am overwhelmed. A perfectly normal day and then...' She stopped herself, enough of that. 'We've had our problems, Inspector. Don't all couples? But we've always sorted them out... How could it have happened?' She appealed directly. 'You are the expert in such matters, Inspector. What's your opinion on his death?'

A question that went to the heart of the matter. She wanted to know where the Inspector was. Was she already thinking accidental death?

'It's too early for opinions, Mrs DeNeuve.'

'But you must have your ideas, Inspector.'

'No more than you have. What do you think happened?'

'I assume that while very drunk, Graham stumbled down to the lake and somehow fell in. Isn't that the most likely explanation?'

'It is certainly one explanation, Mrs DeNeuve. But there are others. The autopsy will ascertain the exact cause of death. And then I can begin to have opinions. In the meantime, I simply have a body in a lake.'

'A body that has consumed a lot of alcohol,' said Vicky. 'Which must lead one to think...' She flapped a hand weakly. 'I am very sorry, Inspector, I simply know my husband better than you do. One of us should have kept an eye on him last night. And then this would not have happened. One simply assumes a particular drunken episode will have the same outcome as all the others.' She dabbed her eyes. 'Please excuse me, Inspector. This is so public. The sins of the family exposed to the world. Our secrets on display. Oh dear. Your investigation is necessary, I am sure. You don't know the family, Inspector, never having met Graham. But there's no doubt in my mind about the cause of my husband's death, but I must allow you to catch up.'

'Thank you, Mrs DeNeuve.' DI Jones had risen. 'One last point. A little thing, really... Do you have a wheelbarrow?'

'No, I don't,' she said in surprise. 'Is it important?'

DI Jones smiled. 'You never know what's important, madam. Or what will lead you up a gum tree. Thank you for your co-operation.' She closed her notebook and put her pen in her inside pocket. 'An area of the lake has been taped off. Scene of crime officers are currently going over it looking for evidence that might assist. The body will be taken away for an autopsy shortly. Then with the pathologist's report on the post mortem, we'll know with some certainty the cause of your husband's death. And then, hopefully, work out how it happened. Time consuming, but necessary, Mrs DeNeuve.'

'You have your job to do, Inspector.'

'I'd be obliged if you stayed away from the taped area. I or one of my officers will keep you informed of any developments. In the meantime, thank you for your help at this distressing time.'

DI Jones left her. Vicky lay back exhausted. She had performed well. The woman was competent, too competent. And that question about the wheelbarrow, that was a shock. With all those officers scouring the lakeside. How thorough had the girls been last night? Everything rested on it. She was unable to move from her armchair. To an outsider, it would appear as if she were immobilised by grief.

Chapter 31

Cathy and Ellie sat on the cane furniture on the patio while their mother was in the house being interviewed. The lawn was very green where Vicky had watered it last night. It was short and neat. She had dead-headed the flowers in the herbaceous border along one side of the lawn. The dahlias were brilliant, the reds, yellows, and oranges flashy and bright. They were Vicky's pride. Every autumn she took the tubers in, wrapped in copies of *The Times,* and put them in the cupboard under the stairs. Then planted them out the following May. Along the other side of the lawn was her rose bed, the pinks, whites, yellows and blood reds in resplendent petal. She was thorough with her feeding and quick with insecticide at any sign of distress.

At the rear of the lawn was the gazebo, made from woven willow, partly obscuring the vegetable garden, where Cathy or Ellie might have seen, if they were looking, a stand of corn, bean poles, and soft fruit.

But they weren't looking at fruit and vegetables.

'This is awful,' said Ellie. 'The game we have to play.'

'Play it well.'

'How cut up we all are.' She waved a hand like a flapper girl, mimicking. 'Oh, oh, how dreadful it is for the family, I'll never get over it, I want to jump into his grave...' She stopped, performance over. 'While the reality is, we filled Daddy up with alcohol through a tube, just in case he wasn't drunk enough, and then carted him down to the lake on a little family trip – where he was dumped like a load of rotten vegetables...' She stared across at her sister. 'He was our father, Cathy.'

Cathy blew a raspberry. 'He was a drunk. Bad enough. How many students that lost us – who can say? He pretended to work, he was a useless headmaster. Bramley was running downhill so fast that the crash was imminent... Two hundred years the school has been in our family. That's the sin that puts him beyond the pale.' She shook a fist. 'We were about to lose it, Ellie.' Her eyes glowed, her hands flashed. 'Alive, he would've bankrupted us with his incompetence.'

'I know, I know,' said Ellie wearily.

Cathy leaned forward and gripped Ellie's arm. 'Don't be the weak one, Ellie. We are all in this together, me, you and Mummy. Daddy is dead. Drunk and drowned. Keep your nerve. The police won't stay long.'

Ellie withdrew her arm from her sister's grip.

'What about George and Jenny Grove?'

'All George has to say to the police is that he saw nothing.'

'He's been here seventeen years, Cathy. He knows all sorts of things about all of us. And what was that with the computers he was shifting this morning? You were in the car park when he was bringing them in.'

'He stole them all!' exclaimed Cathy. 'Complete lack of loyalty. I was watching him take our computers out of his car. I couldn't believe it. The barefaced cheek of the man. He didn't give a damn that I was watching.'

'He does have something bigger on us,' said Ellie.

'He had them in the boathouse all the time...'

'I know.'

'How do you know?'

'Because I looked. I was thinking of taking a boat out,' she said awkwardly.

'With your builder?'

'Mind your own business.'

'It might be a good idea to leave off slumming for the time being.'

'When I want your advice on my love life,' snapped Ellie, 'I'll ask for it. Thank you very much.'

They were silent and seething. Too much history, rows, fights, rages. They couldn't disengage. It was the way they were.

'You were telling me about the caretaker and the computers,' said Ellie, 'before you went off-piste.'

Cathy shrugged. 'He'd put them in the boathouse for the time being, before he could get them away, sell them, I don't know the exact ins and outs, and he was afraid the cops would find them when the body was reported. And so he's put them in the school cellar.'

'Let's hope they don't look there.'

'Why should they?' said Cathy. 'It's death by misadventure. An accident. Why should they be suspicious?'

'Should they find them,' said Ellie determinedly, 'and get George for them, he may well not hold back on what he knows about our little affair. After all, he'll get jailed, get evicted – how could we not evict him for nicking our computers? And then he'll squeal like a stuck pig.'

'He can't move them now,' said Cathy. 'Not with all the cops crawling around. They are where they're staying.'

'What a parade of toy soldiers!'

'Oh shut up!'

'We haven't even preserved Bramley unless this can be sorted out in time... Before the creditors home in. We might have done him in for nothing.'

'Sometimes I hate you, Ellie.'

'Only sometimes, Cathy. That's an improvement.'

The two sisters did not speak a while. Each aware that their fears only led them to attacking each other. Their default for any strong emotion. Bees were buzzing in the dahlias, drinking in the sunlight. A red admiral was hovering above the bean poles.

'Is Mummy still talking to that Detective Inspector?' said Ellie wearily.

Cathy looked in through the French windows.

'No, she's gone.'

'I thought she was going to interview us straight after,' Ellie said. She threw up her hands. 'We can't go anywhere. Stuck like kids in a school detention, until they dismiss us.'

'I'm going in to see Mummy,' said Cathy. 'Find out how she fared.'

'I'm so dog tired, I might have a sleep on the lawn,' said Ellie.

Chapter 32

On the drive to his mother's in Plaistow, Jack and Mia hardly spoke. He tried bringing up the topic of the dead body in the lake, but she was unresponsive, giving him yes and no answers. He thought with Alison in hospital this wasn't the best time for her to find a corpse. Not that there was an ideal time, just some times were easier than others. He wished he knew what was going on with Alison, then at least he could discuss it with Mia, but knowing so little there was not much he could say except admit his ignorance.

And then there was the embarrassment with Ellie. He liked Ellie a lot, and she was up for it. Well, both adults, and the stock cupboard was handy. A bit of fun out of the humdrum, lovemaking mid morning. That didn't come every day. Except it needed to be secret, his and hers. You don't do such things in a school. Above all, you should not be observed by a sharp eyed eleven year old.

And when she'd put him on the spot, he'd told a crass lie.

Traffic was flowing quite quickly on the A12. They went smoothly through Brentwood, all the way to Romford where there was a bit of a hold up, and then picking up again through Chadwell Heath, on the Eastern Avenue. This was one of those journeys that could be 35 minutes or an hour and a half. Depending on traffic. So far so good.

His neck prickled when he thought of the lie he'd grasped from the sky. Why would you go into a stock room, holding hands for heaven's sake, to look at a boy's pictures of horses?

Galloping stallions perhaps.

If there were any pictures, they'd be stacked with other papers on a shelf. You would bring them out into the light anyway.

Lies, illness, death and sex left them with nothing to say. She was looking out the window. Not the most fascinating of roads, a town throughway. How do you get talking again? Find new things to say. He'd have to do something with her. Go out with the telescope, go to the pictures, to the seaside. At least now he was taking her away from the scene.

Normally they got on so well. He'd buggered that par excellence.

From Wanstead, he turned south. Through Forest Gate where he lived, less than two miles from his mother. And two years. Down Upton Lane, and past West Ham Park. Not talking was a strain.

His mother lived on the third floor of a council block near Plaistow station. They took the lift. It smelt faintly of piss. Last time he'd used it the walls had been covered in racist graffiti. At least that had gone. He always worried that the lift would get stuck with him in it. Then they'd have something to talk about.

A total distraction.

She was waiting at the door. It immediately hit him how she had aged. She'd put on weight, her face more lined, the thick purple veins up on the back of her hands. The ginger in her frizzy hair had almost disappeared in grey. Her teeth though had improved, perhaps false. He wondered how she saw him. Would she still be resentful?

'Oh, how you've grown, Mia!'

She ushered them into the flat.

Chapter 33

Susan was nervous as she made the tea, leaving the two of them in the sitting room. She must be on best behaviour. Two years since he was last here. She mustn't mention the money. It didn't matter. It did matter. Such a shameful thing, stealing, she couldn't tell anyone, except Joe. And he'd shrugged it off, but then why should he care? He had already been carrying on with that woman. Not caring was his way of having a go.

In the end, she'd gone to the vicar. And he'd been very good. It was only money, he'd said, and in the scheme of things not a lot of money. Alcohol was the devil incarnate. It took over a soul, made it lie, cheat and steal. We must pray to make his good self stronger. And they had prayed together.

The vicar talked of the prodigal son. The son that had run off and spent everything. Everything but his parents' love. And so when he'd returned they killed the fatted calf for him.

Today, a cream and walnut cake would have to do.

She wanted to rage at her son. For his drunken behaviour, for stealing her money, for two years without contact, for denying her the company of her granddaughter. But she mustn't. He might go away again. But forgiveness was easy to talk about in a Sunday sermon. She wasn't Jesus. She had a sharp tongue, Joe had told her of that. But how could she not be sharp to Joe?

Except it didn't work. Her husband had gone. But then, what good would forgiveness have done? It wasn't the way she was. She couldn't exactly have that woman over for Christmas dinner.

She wouldn't be walked over.

Susan poured the tea into the pot, took a fizzy drink out of the fridge, opened it and put in two coloured straws. She put the teapot and the pop on a tray with a jug of milk. The cake was already on the table. Oh dear, she thought, love was so difficult. She simply wasn't good at it. Her husband ran off, her son too.

Did she expect too much of people?

But you had to have standards, or the world would fall apart. Except she wasn't sure what the standards were. We are all sinners, the vicar said almost every Sunday. And how much can a sinner judge another's sin?

But she did judge. Couldn't help herself. Would die judging.

She took the tray into the sitting room. Jack and Mia were sitting side by side at the table. She'd put on a bright yellow and white table cloth. They were looking at a photo album. One she'd nearly thrown out when Joe left. Mia was laughing at her seven year old dad with a big gap in his front teeth.

'Pop for you,' she said to Mia. 'I didn't think you'd want tea.'

'Thanks, Nan.'

That word almost brought a tear to her eye. It reminded her she was part of a family. Sort of. Fences needed to be repaired. She must try. It would require more than tea and cake.

'How's Alison?' she said as she poured out the tea, and remembered before she'd finished speaking that Jack said they were divorced. Too late.

'She's in hospital,' said Jack.

'Breast cancer,' said Mia.

'It might be,' said Jack more cautiously. 'We're not sure if it's an investigation or more serious...'

'Let's cross our fingers,' she said giving Jack his tea. She took her own. She smiled at her granddaughter sipping through the two straws.

'I saw a body today,' said Mia.

She saw Jack stiffen and thought, play it down. She didn't want a scene.

'Did you, dear?'

'A dead body in the lake,' went on Mia, making it absolutely clear to her Nan what and where.

'She did,' said Jack. 'Where I work. This school. It has a lake.'

'I was bored in the library,' said Mia, 'so I went outside to have a look round. And went down to the lake. And there was this body, floating face down. The headmaster. Wasn't it, Dad?'

Jack nodded. 'It was.'

'And where were you, Jack?'

'I was in the school working...' he began.

'Shouldn't you have been keeping an eye on her?'

'It's a school,' he said vehemently. 'A safe place. You don't expect there to be bodies lying about.'

'It wasn't Dad's fault,' said Mia. 'I was just looking around. He was busy. No one would expect a dead body.'

'Of course not,' she said, retreating. Though she did think he should have been keeping an eye on her. There were always stories about schools in the news, about wicked teachers and caretakers. You don't let an eleven year old wander about on her own in a strange place. Not these days.

'Dad turned him over,' Mia said. 'His face was all white and crinkly, with a snail stuck on the cheek.'

'The police are there now,' said Jack.

'Do you think it was murder, Dad?'

'Probably not. He was very drunk yesterday. I think he probably stumbled in the lake and collapsed. And drowned.'

Susan didn't comment. Drunkenness was a touchy topic. A local drunk had got run over only a week ago. A tenant of her aunt had burnt the house down when drunk and smoking in bed. But it was difficult to know what to talk about with so many touchy subjects.

'Mia is living in Brighton now,' said Jack.

She was relieved at a safe area of conversation. Though she'd gone there with Joe on her last visit to the south coast town, but never mind that.

'Do you like it there, dear?'

And Mia talked about Brighton. About the stony beach, their flat, her school, her friends. And she half listened, watching Jack who was watching her. She cut the cake and gave them both big portions.

Brighton filled a hole. The cake another. But it was a strain. When so much cannot be said... And she was relieved when Jack said he had to get back to work. She could manage Mia, no trouble. A delight. Take her over to the swings, and there was the museum...

Chapter 34

George was out with Buck, keeping him on his lead, or the border collie might run down to the lake where the police were. He was at the top of the hill, watching the activity below, in and around the taped-off area, about the size of a tennis court. Inside it were a man and woman, both wearing white, thin coveralls. They had hats, like shower caps, and gloves of similar material. The woman was on her hands and knees taking a plaster cast of something. The man was searching a patch of grass. Outside the taped area, a uniformed police officer, presumably a guard, stood idly watching him.

An ambulance van was by the lake. Two paramedics in green were placing the corpse on a stretcher.

He wondered whether it was suspicious to watch. Arsonists often joined the crowd to watch the fire brigade putting out the fire. But he was just a man out with his dog, curious. Anyone would be curious. That the body was about to be carried away didn't bother him. That was inevitable. They would take it back to the mortuary, was it? for examination. All that cutting up he'd seen in numerous TV programmes. Cathy had assured him they'd find nothing but alcohol. No cuts or bruises, no bullet wounds. But enough booze to render him a brainless, woozy puppet who had stumbled aimlessly into the water and fallen flat on his face.

The woman making a plaster cast bothered him. What could it be of? Cathy said they'd cleaned the area. Brushed out any prints and scraped it with a board. So what did that leave? The builder and his daughter had found the body, so their footprints would be there. The photographer when he'd come to his house, had photographed the soles of their shoes. He'd seen him do it. So surely there'd be no need to make casts of theirs?

What then?

A print they'd missed. Better not be his. Or hell to buggery, the dog's. That'd be dead easy for Cathy and Ellie to miss. A small dog print. Still, be simple enough to make up a tale for that. All he had to say was he'd taken the dog out last night, let him run free. They might ask him why he hadn't seen the headmaster stumbling about or the body. All he had to say to that was that he just hadn't. He wasn't near the lake, just taking his dog for a walk and minding his own business. The dog had run off, he'd whistled and Buck had returned. Buck might have gone down to the lake, but he hadn't.

Unless they found one of his prints. He knew he should've gone down first thing this morning and done a clean up himself. But he was so wiped out, had hardly slept. No excuse, he shouldn't have left it to the DeNeuve women but done it himself. The only way to be sure.

And the copper scouring the grass? Just looking on the off chance for something, he supposed. Something that might have been dropped. Who knows by whom. But just that little thing that says you were lying. And then they don't believe a word you've said and are all over you.

Even now, they were being so thorough. He hadn't expected all this CSI stuff. Thought they'd come, look at the body and cart it away. And that would be that. Investigation over. Death by misadventure, wasn't that the expression? Not all this palaver with taping off the area, making plaster casts, searching for heaven knows what and questioning everyone. His turn to be grilled pretty soon.

If he'd known it was going to go like this, then he'd have thought twice about agreeing to the cover up. Now he was an accessory. And no matter what he did now, he'd stay one.

He thought he'd been so smart, putting those DeNeuve women on the spot. Job and house back or I spill the beans.

And did he and Jenny have their jobs back? The house? It was just words in the night with three women standing over a body in the lake. They'd agree to anything, caught like that. He needed to get it settled. In writing. Reinstated officially or we go to the law. So he and Jenny could feel secure, start unpacking properly. Instead of just putting a halt to it. He must see Mrs DeNeuve, tell her they needed to know where they were. In writing. Or else.

Or else what? How could he inform on them without incriminating himself? He couldn't. Although, if he did it soon enough, the cops might leave him out of it on the grounds he was a witness who had come to them. But the sooner the better. Must get it in writing, today. No messing. The more time that passed, the more power he gave the DeNeuves. After he'd got the dog back home, he'd go up and see her. And not leave without a letter.

The policeman in the grass had found something. He was standing up and putting something in a plastic bag. The woman making the cast briefly came over to look. Some chat, and they went back to their tasks. The paramedics had laid the body on the stretcher and one of them was putting a belt round it.

This could all be routine. The way they always did things. But the police must believe in the possibility of foul play to be here at all; all it needed was some further hint, something one of them had dropped, conflicting statements – then all their lives, the whole of the school, would be trawled over. And if they got the evidence – then it wasn't just employment and housing at stake, but their freedom too. He must keep calm. They hadn't found anything yet. But how could he be calm with so much in the balance? House, job. Maybe his liberty.

How he wished that he hadn't been out with his dog last night.

And the computers in the basement. There's a complication. Good job he'd been able to get them out of the boathouse. As he'd guessed, the police wanted to look in it. And found nothing to interest them. But there was no way he could move the computers now until they were gone. Not likely they'd look in the basement. Why should they?

Unless they found something. Down there, by the lake.

The two paramedics were lifting the stretchered body. The officer who had been making a plaster cast was directing them, making them go the long way round with their burden, to keep as much as possible out of the crime scene area.

'Hello, George.'

He jerked, surprised at the call. It was Jack, coming over from the car park.

'What's going on down there?' he said, once he'd joined the caretaker.

'A right little beehive,' said George. 'Been there hours. There was another couple for a while. Doing God knows what. They've gone. You do wonder, don't you?' He shook his head. 'A man gets drunk and falls in the water, and how many coppers does it take to find that out? Including a flaming Detective Inspector. Haven't they got any criminals to catch?'

'I am surprised,' said Jack, watching the scene below them. 'Do they do this every time – or have they got a reason for thinking that it wasn't an accident?'

'A load of plods making work for themselves.' He gave the dog lead a jerk. 'Come on, Buck. Let's get you back to the house. I've things to do.' He turned to Jack. 'Cops always make me nervous, no matter what. See you later, mate.'

And man and dog set off.

Chapter 35

Jack went back to his much interrupted job. He was here to make a living and there was no possibility he'd finish today. Not now. There was this door to finish and he hadn't started on the one to the computer room. Sex, death and his daughter had taken him away from his chisel. Back to the doorjamb then. And he was soon chipping out the wood, working symmetrically, hitting the chisel gently with his rubber headed mallet.

Mia had seemed better when he'd left her. She'd even defended him against his mum. Though he was glad to be away. He and his mother couldn't say much with Mia there, and maybe just as well. But they'd met, begun the process which was the main thing. He'd like to just give her the fifty quid and say sorry. Not that he had it. Or that she would accept it.

He had been a drunken bastard. He'd wanted a drink, she had money in her purse. That's all that mattered at the time. There was no future beyond getting well and truly plastered.

But of course there is. Always is. The drunk's solution to everything is to stay drunk. Dissolve tomorrow and every problem in the liquid salve. But then you become the problem, foisted on everyone around you. Alison had ditched him. Changed the locks and divorced him.

Broke, he'd had no choice but to stay sober. He'd spent a week at the Salvation Army hostel until Bob offered him a sofa. And gave him work, but wouldn't give him a penny until he was going to Alcoholics Anonymous. Which didn't work for Jack. Too sanctimonious. All the Twelve Steps twaddle, the higher power mantra which he could do nothing with. What higher power? His mother knew all about it but he'd done with all that when he'd left the church choir as an eleven year old. And he wouldn't fake it for AA.

Alcohol Halt was non religious. Though it picked up its share of AA move-ons who tried to infiltrate the 12 Steps. It depended who was convening on any night, how much was allowed. A crazy place really. A hall full of people who had one thing in common; they were drunks who wanted to stop drinking. The main thing though, he wasn't judged there. Not as a drunk, ex drunk anyway. It was boring, often, but a safe place. A place where he could admit his problem and not be judged for it.

Except it was never quite like that. There was guilt and there was plenty of judgement. Not the fault of Alcohol Halt or the ex drunks who attended. Human nature, you might say. To live is to judge.

Putting down the chisel, Jack tried the lock plate. Not quite. A little needed to come out of the corners. He picked up a smaller chisel and began chipping at the little bits left over.

Ellie. She'd been a surprise. The first words she'd said to him when he first met her reminded him of the Queen. How do you learn to speak like that? he wondered. Of course, if they didn't then you couldn't tell the difference. Which was why they learnt to speak that way. He'd had a mate, a bit of a con man, who'd learnt to speak like a toff. All the better to con you.

Then again, Ellie had this place. Well, her family did. While his estate amounted to a one bedroom flat and a van. But that wasn't so bad considering, not when you compared it to a park bench.

She was exotic in a way. But maybe he'd be to her lot. If he were to ever meet them. But to some of her crowd – he'd be the reverse. Common. Absurd to think of it like that. Judgement again. Blowing up difference to mark out who stood where. All the time.

Would Ellie and he have a fling, as they called it? For it couldn't last. There were rules. There was class. But mostly there was money. If he had the money then he could talk as common as a Billingsgate porter and it wouldn't matter. But he didn't. And it did matter.

Make the most of it, as Bob would say.

The plate fitted. He marked the screw holes, half drilled them. And then screwed down the plate. He closed the door. Nothing stuck. He turned the key in the lock. Smooth.

He'd done one good job today.

Chapter 36

In seventeen years, he'd never come into this room before. What struck him was there was no new furniture in it. Even the sofa he was sitting on could be a hundred years old. For all he knew, two hundred. The table, the sideboard, all the little tables, but if they'd asked him, and they never would, he would say they had too much furniture here. It was like an antique shop. He'd clear half of it out. In the end, furniture was for sitting on or putting things on or in. Not that Jenny would agree with him. She'd probably like this stuff. The curtains were classy, he had to admit that. Long, thick with cords and tassels, nothing cheap there. But the pictures on the walls of their relatives in the lobby, he wasn't sure about that. There were people in his family he wanted to forget as soon as the coffin lid was down. A bit creepy, all those looking down on you, asking, every day, if you are up to it.

When first looking in, seeing the pile of the carpet, it was all he could do to not take his shoes off. He wasn't a servant, he told himself. He'd sat down, gingerly on the edge of the sofa, and they'd given him a coffee. Then talked about the police, what a nuisance they were, their interviews with them and so forth.

All small talk, done for politeness' sake, to get to the point where he could say what he had come here for. Not easy, but he had to say it. And Jenny agreed. It had to be nailed.

What had they to lose? They were either to be thrown out onto the street, lock stock and barrel – or they challenged the DeNeuves. He knew he had a trump card, and it was an ace, but it must be played at just the right moment. One chance they'd get, and he mustn't blow it.

He sipped his coffee. Don't let them frighten you, George. Easy to say. His knees were shaking.

Vicky was in her customary armchair, Cathy sat on the arm of the other, as they chatted as if he were a regular visitor to the big house. There was though an edge, an invisible presence, that all sensed. A murder had been committed, all four of them knew and all four were avoiding the topic. Not much longer. George had to slam it on the table. Or why come here at all?

'I need to know where I am, Mrs DeNeuve.'

She put her coffee on the cork placemat protecting the dark wood table.

'In what respect, Mr Grove?'

No first name, he noted, as it would ever be. But that was neither here nor there.

'With respect to my job,' he said. 'My house, Jenny's job. We have a deal. Don't we?'

Vicky put two fingers to her lips thoughtfully.

'We do and we don't,' she said at last.

'What do you mean?'

He was watching her every move, and keeping a sidelong eye on Cathy who he did not trust an inch. Here, in their domain, were they going to welsh on the deal?

'The police are here,' she said. 'There is an investigation underway...'

'This is all yours now,' he interrupted, his arm indicating her new realm. 'As his wife, you get the lot. You decide who goes and who stays.'

'Yes and no.'

He threw his hands up and sighed.

'Are you going to say that all day, Mrs DeNeuve?'

'Things are not as simple as you want them to be, Mr Grove. You will have to wait a while.'

'I don't get this. I saw her...' he indicated Cathy, 'and her sister drowning Mr DeNeuve last night. And you looking on, like the big boss. Then and there, we made a deal. And I insist that you stick to it.'

'That was before we knew you'd stolen our computers, Mr Grove,' said Cathy.

He turned to her, surprised at her intervention.

'That's got nothing to do with what happened last night.'

Cathy widened her eyes. 'Would you re-employ someone who'd stolen a dozen computers from you?'

'Think what you say before you say it,' he said, teeth gritted, no evasion. 'I saw you murdering your father.'

'I saw you transporting stolen computers,' said Cathy.

He sighed with exasperation. And looked at Vicky secure in her armchair, Cathy hovering like a vulture. How had he ever got stuck with these women?

But he was where he was, in the mire with them.

'I could go out of here and go straight to that Detective Inspector,' he challenged. 'And I could say what I saw last night at the lake.'

'You are an accessory,' said Cathy. 'And a thief.'

'I will deny I had anything to do with those computers,' he said. 'My word against three murderers. And, when it comes to it, they may not be that concerned with me as an accessory, if they want me as the main witness.'

He watched them. It was all on the table. Cathy was barely holding in her anger, her mother tugging at her ear.

'You have it well thought out,' said Vicky.

'I want our jobs back. I want our house back. And I want it in writing,' he said. 'And if I don't get it, then I go straight to that copper.'

'If you do,' said Cathy, 'you'll get no house and no job. And who will ever employ you again?'

George stood up in a fury, his arms flung at them.

'I'll take you down with me, I will. Seventeen years I've been your menial. Yes, Mr DeNeuve, whenever you want, Mrs DeNeuve. Not once have I been in this house. Not even Christmas. I might as well have been a skivvy. Well I tell you this, both of you, may God be my witness, I will risk prison, but I won't be put upon any longer. It's time for respect round here. I've done my job well all my time here. And I've had enough of your insults. I've seen what I've seen. And you know what I've seen. So you write me that letter, Mrs DeNeuve, or I go and see that copper, right now.'

He stood, he waited. He had thrown his ace upon the table. Yes, he would go to the police. It was no bluff. It was the only power he had. They had to know he was serious. Or he had nothing.

Vicky rose.

'Come upstairs to the office, Mr Grove.'

Chapter 37

Jack moved his tools to the computer room, now barren of computers. The room was a little way down the hallway from the classroom where he'd been working. He looked at the broken door, a mess. More damage in the quasi break-in. All done, it was now obvious, by the caretaker, who had the building keys, and had taken the computers and put them in the boathouse temporarily. Then smashed the window and doors to make it look like an outside job.

Did Jack care?

A little. It was a sort of vandalism. At the same time, he had sympathy for George, revenging himself on a heartless employer. He certainly wasn't going to the police. The law might condemn George but there was a cosmic justice in George robbing the people who were throwing him out of house and employment.

Jack would do the repairs and go his way.

The door of the computer room was too far gone. Though the lock could be re-used. He'd need to get the keys for it from George. An irony there. Then he'd repair the doorjamb, again by sawing the damaged part out and replacing it.

He set to, beginning by taking the door off. There was a replacement in the basement, plus the spare wood he needed. That was tomorrow's concern. He put two wedges under the door and with a screwdriver removed the top and bottom hinge. That's when the wedges came into play, taking the weight of the door, stopping it ripping away as the last screws came out. Slowly he eased the remaining screws, his shoulder against the door. They came out without trouble.

He took the door and laid it sideways in the corridor. Coming down it was Ellie. He was instantly charged and found guilty, thinking of the lies he'd told Mia. Pictures of horses... How stupid. He knew that Ellie had come to see him. Why else would she be here? Down, boy. He really needed to get some work done and earn some cash.

She stopped a metre or so away, perhaps wary herself. She had changed her t-shirt and jeans. Blue top, green jeans, her hair washed.

'Been home?' he said.

She nodded. 'After I'd been interviewed, the police said I could go, but wanted me back straight away. I hardly know why. I've told them all I can. How's your daughter?'

'She's at my mother's,' he said. 'A little confused,' he added hesitantly. 'Apart from finding the body, she saw us kissing, and then going into the stock room. I told her we went in to look at some pictures.'

Ellie laughed. 'Good pictures, were they?'

'Pretty good. Though not the best place to keep them.'

'No.' She had darkened.

'You alright?' he said.

'Not really,' she said with a long sigh. 'It's all catching up with me. My father's death... The police. They've taken his body away. I can't understand why they're still here.'

'What do you think happened?' he said.

'An accident. Isn't it obvious? Daddy was drunk. And went out for a walk. I said to him, just the other day, you wander around like that and you'll end up in the lake. Of course he was drunk then too, and it's pointless saying anything to a drunk. He never remembers anything afterwards. Who he's insulted, where he's been. A blank.' She shrugged. 'It was an accident waiting to happen.'

'The police are not sure it was an accident.'

'Did they say that to you?'

'No. But setting up a crime scene... Searching down there, taking plaster casts. You don't do that unless you think there might be some other explanation.'

'It was an accident,' she said firmly. 'That's what they'll come down to.'

'I'm not sure.'

'So what do you think, Mr Holmes?'

He shouldn't have started, he knew at once, the victim being her father, but he'd begun.

'I think the caretaker knows something about it.'

'What?' she shot back.

Now he was out of his comfort zone, putting someone in the frame with the flimsiest of evidence. Hardly evidence at all.

'He knew your father was dead before I told him,' he said.

'How do you know that?'

She was staring at him, trembling. He should not have started this.

'The way George was,' he said. 'His eyes. He was trying so hard to convince me it was an accident...'

'Like I've been?' she said, her eyes wide.

'I didn't mean that.' He was itchy round the neck and took a breather for a rethink. 'After we found the body, I went to see him first, to leave Mia there, so I could tell your mother. And I swear, he already knew your father was dead.'

'I'm not sure where this is going, Jack.' She was agitated, striding about, swinging her arms. She turned back on him. 'Let's suppose George did know, for argument's sake. It doesn't mean he killed my father.'

'But why lie about it? And think about it, he had the best of motives. He and Jenny hated him.'

She threw her hands up. 'Stop, stop, Jack. This is all baseless. You could be totally wrong. You have nothing but your feelings to go on.' Her hands rushed to her cheek, an urgent thought. 'You haven't told the police?'

'Of course not.'

'Then don't. It's all supposition. Amateur detective stuff. Leave it to the professionals.'

He nodded. She was more than likely right. It was all a feeling, and feelings can be utterly wrong. He should have kept his suspicions to himself.

'Sorry,' he said. 'It was tactless of me. You're right. They'll probably conclude it was an accident.'

'What else can it be?' she said. 'When they cut him open, they'll find him loaded to the gunnels with booze.'

Jack's phone rang. He took it from his pocket.

'Excuse me,' he said. 'It's my daughter. I'll keep it short.' He turned away, 'Hello, Mia.'

'Hello, Dad.'

'What's it like at Nan's?'

'We went to this park. They've got a bird house and a butterfly greenhouse. Had ice creams and cake. Can I stay the night? Nan wants to take me to a play a friend of hers is in. An Agatha Christie crime thing.'

'Of course you can stay. I'll see you tomorrow then. Now I must get back to work...'

'You on your own, Dad?'

'Course I am.'

'Not with that lady again?'

'What do you think I am? I'm on my own,' he said, 'in the middle of a job. I've got to earn some money, you know. I haven't done much today, what with the police...'

'And that lady.'

'So I just have to get back to work. Enjoy the play. You can tell me all about it tomorrow. Bye, Mia.'

'Bye, Dad.'

Jack switched off and put the phone back in his pocket.

Ellie came up to him and poked him in the chest. 'On your own – are you?'

'Kids!'

He put his arms round her and they embraced. A long kiss.

'And you're on your own tonight, I hear,' she said in a break. 'Want company?'

Chapter 38

Jenny was in her elder son's room. She was wearing a long blue dress that she'd almost torn up for rags. And maybe would when all this was sorted out. Whenever that might be. The walls in the room were stripped of posters, the single mattress bare. The floor was packed with plastic bags, cardboard boxes and tea chests, full with juvenile paraphernalia, books and clothing.

She took a plastic bag and upturned it on the bed. Out came an assortment of underwear and socks. She opened a drawer and put them in. Not bothering for neatness, just in. She tipped out another bag; this one of t-shirts and sweaters, opened a second drawer and put the clothes back in the same drawer they'd come out of a day earlier.

Get them in, sort them out later. How she longed to be rid of all these boxes and bags. To have a home once more. Bare walls and empty drawers were so dispiriting. She wanted her house back.

George came in with two mugs of tea. He handed her one.

'What a palaver!' he said, looking about him.

She sat on the bed with hers. He was by the door gazing at a room that had lost its familiarity.

'It's like digging holes and filling them in again,' he sighed.

'I am so demoralised,' she said.

'But it's ours again, love.'

'Is it?'

'It's in writing. We are fully re-instated. Jobs and home. Two years, the letter says.'

She shuddered. 'I just don't trust the DeNeuves. It's all given so grudgingly. Well, not given at all. You blackmailed them.'

'I wouldn't call it that.'

'What else is it?'

He didn't speak for a while, but sat on a hard chair, drinking his tea. She had her back to him, sunken.

'They hate us,' she said to the bare window. 'That's what kills me. Living and working where the boss hates you.'

'What choice do we have?' he said. 'He gave us a month's notice on our jobs and the house. A month! The bastard. Now at least, we can look around. One of us find a job, then the other, then see if we can sort out somewhere to live. Say over 18 months. We've got a two year cushion. Not have everything thrown at us like an avalanche. And oh yes, they'll give us brilliant references. Just to see the backs of us.'

'It's better to be in than out, I suppose.' She patted his hand. 'That's got to be so. But I can't dance for joy when I see all this lot,' she indicated the boxes and bags all around, 'two weeks to get this far. And now we have to unbundle them, just to be where we were. Correction. Not quite where we were. Here on sufferance.' She turned to her husband. 'Facing the evil eye every day.'

'I know that alright. I had it up at the house. They'd love us away from here and forgotten.'

He punched a fist into a palm.

'You're a witness, George,' she said. 'They've killed the head. They'd love to see you dead too.'

'But I'm not drunk and helpless. By God, I'm not.'

She sighed. 'I wonder whether we might just be better off going. We haven't cancelled that place yet...'

'That hole in the wall. No way are we going there.'

'But we'd be obliged to no one. Not like here. We've got some savings.'

'No. We are staying, Jenny. We have two years to sort out somewhere. Don't let them push us around. We'll get ourselves unpacked and we'll stay. On our terms, till that contract runs out. Chin up, love. They can't push us around anymore. We are here. Whether they like us or not. We'll do our jobs and we'll stand our ground.'

'They hate our guts.'

'It's mutual. No pretending now. But we'll get respect. We insist on that. Respect. No doormat treatment from now on.'

'What are you going to do with those computers?'

'Bloody things. I'd put them back if I could, but they've been reported stolen. I wish I'd never taken them. But how was I to know that this was going to happen? I thought, get something out of Bramley after 17 years. Anyway, they're safe in the cellar. There's no reason for the cops to go down there. And as soon as they're gone, I take them to the dealer.'

The silence engulfed them, the boxes and bags pressing on them like added gravity.

'I should be pleased,' she said. 'We're back. You got us two years. But I'm just tired.'

He put a hand on her shoulder. 'It's the boxes, love. It's the strain. The quicker we get unpacked, the quicker we get some heart back.'

'Whatever we do, George,' she said, 'it's not ours. And that's the truth of it. Sooner or later, we've got to go.' She closed her eyes. 'I want to live somewhere where we are not despised.'

'Who wouldn't?' said George. 'But we haven't got that choice. I am the caretaker of Bramley again. You are catering manager. This is a damned good house. And it's ours. For the time being.'

Chapter 39

The DeNeuves were in the garden, on the patio. Vicky had done a little dead heading in the herbaceous border. She wanted to hoe the vegetables, but Cathy had insisted on a family chat before she went home. Another one. It had been such a long day, two packed into one. She'd hardly slept the night before, what with all the busyness at the lake. You don't simply snooze till morning, having killed your husband. It was so engulfing, she wished the day done with. Presumably, one in time got used to the facts as they now were, and lived as one used to, but sans husband. A widow, accustomed to her widowhood.

'What are we going to do about Mr Grove?' said Cathy.

'Nice dog he's got,' said Ellie. 'But I'd rather not have seen it last night.' She was stirring the lemon and ice in her elderflower cordial.

'He came here,' said Vicky sipping her drink, 'like Caesar demanding tributes.'

'Which we promptly gave him,' exclaimed Cathy. 'He made a fool of us. A caretaker for God's sake. He simply came here, demanded his job back and that of his stupid wife, and his house. *His* house! And we caved in.'

'We didn't have much choice,' said Vicky. 'What do you say, Ellie?'

'Serves us right, I suppose. Daddy sacked and evicted them in one fell swoop. What would you do in their position?'

'Have you been talking to your builder again?' said Cathy.

'His name is Jack.'

'And he's standing up for the rights of the working man... Soon we'll have the unions here, picket lines before you know it.'

'I was just putting myself into George Grove's shoes, Cathy. I know it's not usual in mathematics but we do it in English literature all the time.'

'He's not Othello, he's a bloody caretaker!'

Vicky poured herself another cordial, avoiding the lemon slices accumulating in the jug.

'He's getting very bolshie, I must say,' she said. 'He gave us an ultimatum, a letter of reinstatement or he'd go straight to the police. And I had the feeling he would.'

'In spite of the fact he'd get in trouble himself?' queried Ellie.

'In spite of it.'

'That's a lot of resentment,' said Ellie.

'I don't think we need write an essay on his character,' said Cathy. 'What are we going to do about him?'

'I'm sure they are unpacking right now,' said Vicky.

'As if the house was theirs!' exclaimed Cathy. 'I shudder what they've done to the place.'

'Well, we know what to do. We either kill him or live with him for two years,' said Ellie. 'That's not forever.'

'Two years in which he will not take orders, my simple sister. He'll do what he damn well wants. He'll walk all over us.'

'So what's your suggestion?' said Ellie.

'I simply know you can't have employees ruling the roost! Bramley is ours. Not theirs. Suppose...' She thought for an instant. 'I ask him to polish the hall floor. He says he doesn't feel like it. What do I do then?'

'Polish it yourself?' said Ellie with a chuckle she made no attempt to hold back.

'Oh shut up, you little slummer!'

'A little manual work wouldn't hurt us once in a while...'

'Where are you coming from? This is an independent school. What would parents think if they saw me or you polishing the school floors?'

'In that suit?' said Ellie. 'Now I know why you never take it off. In bed, even?'

Cathy threw her hands in the air. 'This is a waste of time. She refuses to see the situation, Mummy. Where we are. What this does to us. As if nothing at all has changed.'

They were silent, jiggling ice cubes, thinking about themselves, their father, Bramley and a caretaker who had too much power.

'Kill him or live with him. We haven't really got beyond that,' said Vicky. 'Though I wonder how legal that letter is. Might it be worth going to a solicitor with it?'

'Not just yet, Mummy,' said Ellie.

'No,' she said, 'but after the inquest and cremation... And if the solicitor says it's not contractual then we fire him.'

'And if the solicitor says it is contractual?' said Cathy. 'Or the Groves take us to a tribunal?'

'He'd get a lot of sympathy,' said Ellie. 'The underdog in a tied house, with a bully of an independent school taking home and job away, in spite of the letter signed by you...'

'He could get a lot of money out of us,' sighed Vicky, 'if we go that road. Damn the man. We may simply have to live with him for the term of the letter. Then... and only then, we terminate.'

Ellie laughed. 'You might yet be polishing the hall floor, Cathy. And pregnant too. That will be a sight come December.'

'Oh God,' moaned Cathy. 'Live with that prick for two years. He will take such pleasure in tormenting us. We might as well not have a caretaker for all the work he'll do.'

'Have you another tactic?' said Vicky.

'I simply know I will not be humiliated.'

Chapter 40

Ellie shook herself. She had nodded off. And for a moment wasn't sure where she was. Her classroom, at her desk. Her laptop open in front of her, showing the screensaver of a dancing coloured ball. How long had she been out? At least ten minutes for the screensaver to cut in. She wriggled her neck and rubbed the top of her shoulders. Her energy came in waves today. One moment hyper, the next dopy, drifting off. The builder had been a hyper moment, can't have been long since she was with him outside the computer room. Flooded with energy. Must be adrenaline. Fight or flight. Sex. She hoped it wasn't too obvious. But what if it was?

He was sharp for a builder. Oh, what a snobby thing to think! Why should a builder be stupid? You have to be able to use tools, select the right materials, calculate. Just because he didn't go to University – as Cathy might say. He was good looking and he challenged her. Mostly she liked that, verbal fencing, but not when it came to what happened to her father and the caretaker's connection. Jack had picked up that George was lying. She just hoped she'd put him off. Or had he picked up on her? Her lies.

This dreadful business.

She half laughed, thinking of Cathy in the garden. Was she really contemplating killing the caretaker? When you've done one, the next is easier – they say. The tenth a doddle. She became quite stupid with Cathy around. Had to beat her, at all costs. No matter that the real problem was the caretaker. Yes, he had a hold on them. But at the meeting it was Cathy. Cut her, insult her. Never mind the business on hand. So childish. But she would not back down. Not with her sister, who would only see it as weakness.

Ellie massaged her shoulders and the back of her neck. She should move, stuck in her chair. Not the best place to nod off. She looked about the classroom, at the bare walls. And sighed, so much to do before the start of term. Displays to go up, the curricular work which Cathy had already completed. But it wasn't going to get done today. She was utterly washed out. Jack had gone, so no more hyper moments with him, until she got to his place in a couple of hours. She wondered how he lived. His flat. Slumming as Cathy put it. Well, soon she'd find out.

Ellie shook herself. She'd nodded off again. Would she be alright to drive home? Perhaps she should get a taxi. So little sleep... None actually. How can you when you've just drowned your father? The three of them, teamwork at last. Topping him up with booze, getting him out of the house and into the wheelbarrow, into Cathy's car and down to the lake. They should have had a picnic. Got a boat out. A champagne send off.

Why was she dwelling on this?

So whacked out, her mind was wandering. She should leave and get home before Clive got back. She didn't want to see him, he didn't want to see her. Now that Daddy had gone, she could move in with Mummy. That wouldn't be bad for a month or two. Get away from Clive, get the flat sold. Of course, she couldn't bring anyone back to Mummy's. But Jack had his own place. He was awfully nice, and the fact that Cathy thought him unsuitable made him even nicer.

She'd best pick up some food for tonight. No matter what his other skills were, she didn't believe he could cook.

'Hello.'

Ellie looked up and saw Detective Inspector Jones at the classroom door. She was dressed disturbingly like Cathy in a dress suit, but had a cockney accent, which made Ellie think she'd probably worked her way up through the ranks. No family connections. Which meant she was good. Or slept with the Chief Constable.

'Can I help you?' said Ellie, trying to look awake.

'Yes, you can. I'm looking for Mr DeNeuve's office.'

Ellie was immediately switched on again. Thinking. Give nothing away. Be helpful.

'I'll take you there,' she said.

As they walked down the corridor, Ellie said, 'Will you be here much longer, Inspector?'

'We've nearly all we want,' said DI Jones. 'We'll be out of your hair tomorrow.'

'It's lucky...' began Ellie, and instantly bit her tongue. What was lucky about your father dying? 'Another few weeks and it would have been very inconvenient.'

Heavens! What was she saying? Investigating her father's death – inconvenient!

'I know,' said DI Jones. 'School holidays. Easier for us too.'

'Have you come to any conclusions?'

'There's no obvious injuries on the body,' said DI Jones. 'But there'll be a full autopsy in the next couple of days. Then a date for an inquest will be set...'

'So there will be an inquest?'

'Definitely.'

'But isn't it obvious how he died?'

'I have my own ideas, Miss DeNeuve, but there are a few worrying elements – which is why I want to see your father's office.'

Ellie wanted to ask about the worrying element. But didn't feel she could. Was not enough in charge of herself to dare.

They came to the office. Ellie knew the push-button code and opened up.

A smell of whisky hit them as they entered. An empty bottle lay on the floor by the large desk whose top was strewn with doodled papers, a folded Times with the crossword half done, a chain of paperclips, and, somewhat incongruously, Book V of *Caesar's Gallic Wars*. Ellie looked closer at the newspaper, it was yesterday's. She felt sick, as if her father was sitting there, accusing her. She didn't trust herself. She was trembling, breathing quickly.

'This is very disturbing,' she said, shuddering. 'Do you mind if I leave you here, Inspector?'

'Of course not,' said the Inspector, beginning to look at the papers on the table. 'I completely understand.'

'I feel sick.'

Ellie rushed out the door almost hitting the doorjamb, down the corridor, holding her mouth and stomach, gagging. She scrambled into the toilet, into a cubicle, put her head in the pan. And vomited.

Chapter 41

Jack began with the washing up. In the morning he usually just piled it all in the sink before he went out to work. Sometimes he did the same in the evening until he ran out of crockery, which wasn't that long as he didn't have much. He thought it practical not to buy any more. It would only make him messier.

The kitchen floor could do with a wash. The thought was easily dismissed; they weren't going to eat off it. Not so easily, the stove top. It was filthy. Dark brown grease with small helpless islands of white enamel between. Mostly he didn't see it, just added to it with his fry ups. But with someone coming, he must clean it. Somewhat.

He begrudged doing it. Such a waste of time, scrubbing and washing. It would only get dirty again.

OK, twenty minutes. Strict. And he stuck to it. Clock watching. Scouring and scraping until the time was up. It was twenty minutes cleaner. Better. He wondered what Ellie was used to. Did she scrub her kitchen cooker? Wash her floors? No, she'd have a cleaner.

He'd ask her.

He ran around his sitting room, gathering up papers, take-away boxes, an overfull bin, and took them all to the outside dustbins. Then spent five minutes searching for the vacuum cleaner. In a flat this size it should be easy to find, except it was buried in a cupboard. It was a sweat getting it out. And almost put him off using it. But there it was, mid carpet, accusing. Use me.

He began vacuuming the sitting room; not much suction. The bag was almost full. He wasn't going to empty it, besides he didn't have any spare bags. But the room did need a sweep... He emptied the bag onto newspaper, choking in the dust. The old bag was well past its sell by date. He put it back on and crossed fingers it wouldn't split while he did the sitting room.

He used to clean up regularly. When Alison had lived in London, she'd come over once and told him straight – Mia wasn't coming to a filthy flat. He'd argued, on principle, even though he knew she was right. So he cleaned before Mia next came. Alison had conceded it was better. But warned him that if he slipped, then no Mia. So he cleaned whenever Mia was coming over. But then Alison and Mia moved to Brighton. And he'd slipped back as Alison no longer came to inspect.

Maybe one day she'd do a surprise inspection. Just to catch him out.

Mia sometimes complained. And they did a clean up together. There were other times, like now, when he had someone coming. He shuddered to think how he'd live if he had no guests.

Squalor. Like those old people, found dead after a year, a rotting corpse in a house stuffed full of rubbish. Would that be his end? Dying alone, in a mess.

He only cleaned up for other people. Better keep them coming.

Jack went into the bedroom. Another room that would be used. Thankfully, he had a clean bed-sheet in the cupboard. That went on. He smelt the duvet cover. Acceptable. He had another but it was in the dirty washing. One clean pillowcase. He felt sure he had a pair. The other in the same place as all those lost socks. Sucked down a wormhole into a universe which consisted entirely of lost socks, ballpoints, library books, engagement rings, lost promises, hopes and dreams...

He put the one pillowcase on, the other he turned inside out and slipped back on. Then Jack sat down, more exhausted than from a day's work.

Ellie had phoned earlier. She was bringing some food. That was a relief. He had hardly anything in and was short of cash after filling up the van earlier. Still, the job would be finished tomorrow and with luck he'd get paid cash on the spot.

Freed from chores, he could think about Ellie. It had come out of nowhere, their scene. He would never have imagined it, not with someone so posh... Her accent, like a lady-in-waiting. Her father had just ignored him. Walking past him in the corridor, that severe way of not looking, passed on through the generations. Didn't Victorian servants have to turn to face the wall when their betters came down the corridor?

Ellie was educated, while he couldn't wait to leave school. Still, he'd met plenty of stupid, educated people, who'd read no end of books but couldn't change a washer. She had money and had a father who could sack a caretaker with the flick of his fingers.

Maybe that's why he was dead.

He and Ellie differed about George. In the van coming home he'd reverted to his old opinion. George was lying. George was somehow involved in Mr DeNeuve's death. He was almost sure of it. The 'almost' was irritating. George had stolen the school computers, sure enough. Ellie had said that didn't make him a killer.

That couldn't be argued with.

George was involved though. He'd go that far. Maybe not killed him. Or maybe he did. Job and home were pretty good motives.

Suppose Mr DeNeuve had gone for a wander in the middle of the night, left his house still tipsy, maybe had topped himself up on his wanderings. Then collapsed somewhere in the grounds. And then along comes George, sleepless, worried about their impending move and his unemployment, finds him passed out on the path, the cause of all their troubles. So easy to give him another wheelbarrow ride; this one down to the lake. And tip him in.

Well, it was a story. With no evidence for the beginning, or the middle, and just a corpse in the lake at the end. And a lying caretaker somewhere in it. Or a mistaken builder.

Leave it to the professionals, said Ellie. Yeh, they had the body, were crawling all over the crime scene. Had interviewed everyone. Leave it to them, like she said. Except he was on the spot. He'd barrowed DeNeuve home last night, and with Mia found him in the morning. The cops came in cold.

Forget it.

He shouldn't play the wise guy and try to teach the cops their job.

A look at his watch, and Jack did another trip round the flat, as if Ellie might come in, turn her nose up and leave. He'd chance the vacuum cleaner. And did the bedroom, opening the window to air it, and decided that was most definitely that.

He picked up an astronomy magazine. And thought he must get out soon with the telescope. Last night with Mia was clouded over. Today the sky was clear, still pretty clear now, but he had other business tonight. But maybe tomorrow. Mars was well placed and the moon a good fallback.

His bell rang.

Chapter 42

Ellie's initial plan had been to make a meal at Jack's. She enjoyed cooking. It didn't have to be complicated. Fish, some salad, summer fruit and ice cream. She'd gone into Waitrose, picked up a wire basket to fill with the various ingredients and was suddenly overwhelmed with tiredness. No way could she cook. She'd fall asleep over the frying pan. And she put the basket back and walked out empty handed.

She wondered if she should be going to Jack's at all. In this state. Wouldn't it be better to just flop? Except she desperately wanted company. And Clive was no longer in the running. Simply an indifferent presence. Worse. She wanted to be held, told that she mattered.

She had to get through the next couple of days. Into normality. Back to routine. Her classes. Teaching, getting the children under control, asking for homework, sorting out their personal problems. Busy, busy.

And in the meantime, Jack was here. Was she using him? Of course, though she never knew why that was wrong. He wanted it, she wanted it. She would never marry him. He knew that, she knew that. Although it would so annoy Cathy if she did. There was no Daddy to storm and rant anymore. That was a curious freedom, the thought that she could marry him.

She'd only known him two days! And here was she drawing happy families.

Not if he knew she'd drowned her father. Would that be grounds for divorce, that she hadn't told him she had murdered, part murdered Daddy? Might their daughter, some thirty years hence, cart her down to the lake at Bramley? And tip her in.

It would serve her right if she did.

What a scenario! Lack of sleep was driving her whacky.

Today, she'd travelled around by taxi and train. No driving. First dropped off at home. Clive wasn't there, thank heavens. A shower, clean clothes and another cab to Brentwood Station. There she'd caught the train to Stratford as per Jack's instructions, and then another to Forest Gate. There was a Co-op supermarket next door to the station, but after a minute or two walking around the shop blankly, she remembered she wasn't going to cook. She recalled an Indian restaurant she'd seen across the road from the station. She retraced her steps and crossed the high street, to the restaurant, where she ordered a meal to be delivered.

She picked up a bottle of plonk and, consulting her *A to Z*, headed for Jack's. Quite a lively area, the street lights just coming on. Takeaways, lots of betting shops – was that what working people did when they weren't at the pub? What a mass of prejudices she was. Strollers of all age and hue on the street. She'd never been to Forest Gate before. Been warned off by people who'd never been here either. All shootings and drugs gangs, they'd said. No one was shooting anyone tonight that she could see, though half her dozy mind wouldn't say no to a bullet. Providing it went to the dead centre of the brain.

At Jack's, a welcome embrace. The flat was small, tidier than she'd expected. It reminded her of her student days.

'We've an Indian meal on the way,' she said. 'I hope it works out. I ordered it at Aromas, just near Forest Gate station.'

'Quite good, that place,' said Jack with approval. 'Mia and I've eaten there a couple of times.'

'I was going to cook something,' she said, excusing herself, 'I love cooking, but today has been such a strain – I simply couldn't face it.'

'Fine by me.'

'I will make you a meal,' she said. 'Promise. Just not tonight.' She held up the bottle of wine. 'Drink?'

Jack hesitated, then said, 'I don't drink. Sorry, Ellie, should've told you. I'm on the wagon. I mustn't touch the stuff. I don't mind if you do.'

Ellie twisted the cap off. Cheap plonk, no cork. She took it into the kitchen, and she poured it down the sink.

He came in, to see her holding the empty bottle.

'You didn't have to do that.'

'I did,' she said. 'My father was a drunken bully who ended up drowned in the lake... Just suppose he'd have sworn off this stuff, he'd still be here.' She washed the bottle out and put it on the side. 'I took the Detective Inspector to Daddy's office this afternoon. The place stank of whisky. On the floor was an empty bottle, the one that did for him I expect. I don't know what he had in his cupboards, probably more stash. I could see him at his desk drinking, yelling into the phone, charging into Mummy's room and tearing strips off her... I felt sick and had to run away.' She gave a half smile. 'I don't need to drink tonight, Jack. I've got you.'

She kissed him on the cheek. And he enfolded her.

'Oh, I need you,' she sighed.

Her energy was back. Food first. She escaped the embrace and set the table. Pity there was no table cloth. It was just like a student flat. She put out the cutlery, a jug of water and two glasses. And thought it was sound to get rid of the booze. With Jack not drinking, that would have left her with the whole bottle. Pissed, who knows what she might have admitted?

The doorbell rang. She went down, knowing it was their food. There was far too much, in two carrier bags, the separate items in foil dishes. She placed them out: the meat dishes, the vegetables, the popadoms, the naan, the rice, the oddments.

'I always do this,' she said. 'I get tempted, I don't want to miss out on anything. Anyway, I'm sure you have a good appetite.'

'I do,' he said. 'I haven't eaten since lunchtime. In fact, I'm glad you didn't cook.'

'I'm quick,' she said, slightly hurt.

'What did I say that for? Sorry. I am sure you're an amazing cook.'

'You'd better believe it. Now dig into this lot. And you can't go till it's finished, as my father might have said.'

They began with the popadoms and dips.

'Cathy went home just before I left,' she said, 'and that left Mummy all alone.' She sighed. 'I should have kept her company, but I couldn't stand another evening there.'

'It's been a rough day.'

'I'm going to be poor company,' she said. 'I shall be morose, tearful, sulky. And what hurts a man most of all – I won't laugh at your jokes.'

'At the moment,' he said, 'all I want to do is to eat and look at you across the table. And decide when to eat you too.'

'I think you'd best start with the food, Mr Wolf. It's not so nice cold.' She looked about the flat. 'You own this place?'

'Yes,' he said. 'This flat, my van and tools. My worldly wealth.'

'It looks alright to me,' she said helping herself to curry and vegetables. 'You don't seem unhappy.'

'I'm OK now,' he said. 'Getting by. Building work is an up and down game though. You never can be sure you'll get work.'

'The DeNeuves have always had too much,' she said. 'It isn't good for you. You get scared. As if it would be Armageddon to lose Bramley... But it might in fact be one hell of a release.' She took some peas and cauliflower. 'Our family was born with its nose in the air. Always believing we were better than hoi polloi. And secretly afraid that we weren't really.'

'It's all relative,' said Jack. 'This place would be riches to someone sleeping on the street.' A sudden thought. 'Have you got a cleaner?'

She smiled at the switch of subject. 'Yes, I have. I mean Clive and I have. Maria comes in twice a week. It'd be a tip otherwise.' She held her hands up. 'But let's clear things up. I'm not doing the dirty on Clive tonight by coming here. He's past caring. We simply share a flat because we're too lazy to move on. It's not a relationship. We don't talk. We shout, if we bother at all. Besides, I've decided to move back in with Mummy. It'll be alright there now, with Daddy gone. And she needs the company.'

His phone rang.

Jack looked at it. 'It's my mother, I'd better answer it. I'll make it quick.'

'Hello, Mum,' he said, and went into the kitchen, closing the door after him.

Ellie tore off a piece of naan. She spooned some mutton dopiaza onto her plate, some saag aloo and various bits and pieces. She was glad the food worked out. A poor meal could ruin an evening. Especially this early in a relationship. But this was good. She took another biteful and savoured. Yes, good. And her energy was back. Who knew how long for? But she was here, now. And Jack was energising company. Perhaps not right for marriage. Not when it comes to property. And like Mrs Bennet, one should be practical in terms of money and property. But it wasn't 1805, and she could have her fling. However long it lasted. A body to comfort her. To pass the night with. X nights with. To help her get over the black days.

Though she should be with Mummy. So should Cathy. In fact, she hadn't realised Cathy wasn't going to be there tonight, before setting things up with Jack. Vicky said she'd be fine. She'd have a quiet house for once. No drunks stumbling in late.

There was George of course, the uppity caretaker. Surely it wasn't in his interest to spill the beans. Cathy could be awfully dramatic. It would subside. Just these first days to endure.

She wouldn't have minded some wine now. A cool glass of red. She was used to it with food. And with sex. But a whole bottle to herself? No, just as well it was gone. She needed to keep control of her tongue.

Jack returned.

'My daughter, Mia, had a terrible nightmare,' he said. 'She's crying uncontrollably.'

'She found the body,' said Ellie, recalling. 'It's delayed reaction. I've seen it before in kids. They can be fine for a few hours after some crisis, then it hits them. Wham!'

'I've got to go over there,' he said, a hand on her shoulder. 'Sorry.' He kissed her on the cheek. 'It's not every day my daughter finds a dead body. I'll be back. I won't stay any longer than I need to. Eat, watch TV, read my magazines...'

'Buzz off,' she said. 'And hurry back.'

He grabbed his jacket and left. His feet padded down the stairs, the street door banged.

She sighed. Abandoned. With all that food. But her appetite had gone, swept out the door with Jack. Energy too. She felt sunk into the ground.

Sex was rarely simple. Life intervened. She and Clive had met on holiday in the south of France. Sex and beach, more sex, more beach, wine and good food. Then, but only then, it was simple. Until they came off holiday and moved in together. Then moods and demands took over. Work. His bloody mother.

She felt drowsy again. Maybe she'd have a nap. She hoped Jack wasn't long. She needed warmth. Flesh. Words to match her words. Connection.

She couldn't face her own company.

Chapter 43

Mia was in winceyette pyjamas that his mother had borrowed from a neighbour. She looked younger on the sofa at his side, huddled round her cocoa. His mother was in her long dressing gown and slippers, her grey hair frizzy.

'She came running into my room,' said his mother. 'Screaming and yelling – my mother's dead! My mother's dead! I couldn't quieten her down. Crying. Oh, what a state you were in, poor thing.'

'It was a terrible dream, Daddy.'

He put his arm round his daughter. 'Tell me about it.' Wasn't that the thing to do? Talk about the thing bothering you. Or alternatively talk about anything but.

'I saw a body in a lake,' she said. 'In the dream. And I went down the hill towards it. I couldn't stop myself. I didn't want to. But I had to. And just as I got to the side of the lake, there was this big wave on the water, and the body turned over. And it was Mum. She was all horribly white with a snail on her cheek.'

'Oh, that's a dreadful dream,' exclaimed Jack. It barely needed interpreting. All the things that were worrying her.

'She is alright?' said Mia. 'Mum?'

'She's fine,' said Jack. 'I spoke to her earlier.' He hadn't, but it was a comforting lie. There was no way they could phone the hospital now. 'You can phone her in the morning.'

'I prayed,' said his mother, 'when I couldn't calm her down. And that told me to phone you.'

'I'm glad you did,' he said, thinking of Ellie back at his flat on her own. But what could he do? He wasn't the best of fathers. It had been a screw up this morning, which was why he'd come running over.

'That lady was in my dream,' said Mia.

'What lady?' said Jack. And at once, in the presence of his mother, regretted asking.

'The one I saw at the lake yesterday,' said Mia.

'I don't understand you, Mia. What lady, where?'

'I saw this lady down by the lake,' she said.

'Is this the dream?' said Jack.

'Yes, in the dream, but also real. When I went out for a wander this morning, I was up the hill looking down on the lake. And there was this lady. She had a board in her hand. And when she saw me, she ran away. It was then I went down to the shore and saw the body and phoned you.'

'You never told me about any lady,' said Jack.

'I was angry with you,' she said, 'about you know what. So I never said.'

'Did you tell the police?'

'No, I forgot.'

'What d'you mean you forgot?'

'They didn't ask me. And I forgot to say.'

'You can't just forget something like that, Mia.'

Mia cowered and screwed up her eyes.

'Jack, please,' said his mother.

'I'm sorry,' said Jack. 'It's alright if you forgot. It's horrible seeing a body. Anyone might forget. I bet I would.' He mustn't shout at her, poor kid. She'd had a nightmare for heaven's sake. 'What did the lady look like, Mia?'

'She was wearing a baggy track suit. It was much too big for her. She looked a bit like that lady, you know. But it can't have been her. Can it?'

'No,' said Jack quickly, knowing exactly where Ellie had been.

He should phone the police. But he'd come here for Mia. And Ellie was waiting back at his place. This had to be one hundred per cent fatherhood. Forget anything else.

'Your mother is fine,' he said. 'And the police are investigating the body in the lake. We'll leave that all to them.'

'There were three bodies in the play we saw,' said Mia.

'What play?'

'The Agatha Christie we saw. I told you. Anyway. One was poisoned, one was stabbed and the third was hit on the head with a candlestick.'

'What a suitable play for you!' exclaimed Jack.

'I'm sorry,' said his mother. 'I just didn't think.'

'Neither did I,' said Jack. 'That's a lot of bodies for an eleven year old. But at least three of them were only acting.'

'It must be difficult to act dead,' said Mia. 'Do you have to hold your breath?'

His mother laughed. 'No. On stage you can breathe. The audience can't see that close. But in a film, you have to hold your breath when the camera's on you.'

'But you have to stay absolutely still on the stage,' said Mia. 'I was watching the man murdered in the library. He was lying there with a knife in his back for ages and ages. And I was watching and watching to see if he moved. And he didn't, not at all.'

'I bet he really wanted a speaking part,' said Jack.

'He did have a speaking part,' said Mia. 'To begin with. He was this nasty colonel, shouting at everybody, especially his daughter. I'm glad he got murdered.'

Jack smiled. He looked at his mother who was also smiling.

His mother said, 'Isn't it odd, how we like murder in a play or a film. A good gruesome killing. But we'd hate to come across it in real life.'

'Well, no one died tonight at the theatre,' said Jack. 'And I think it's time we got off the subject. We've done it to death, you might say. How are we going to get this one back to bed?'

'You could read to me, like you used to,' said Mia. She picked up a book beside her. 'I borrowed this from the school library.'

'You didn't.' He took it from her, a little shocked. It was a thick Harry Potter. He opened it. Inside was printed Bramley Independent School. He shrugged, well, it was the least they could provide, given Mia's experience at the school.

He took his daughter back to her bedroom. And there by the light of a reading lamp, he read a few chapters of *Harry Potter and the Half-Blood Prince*. At which point, Mia was very drowsy and asked him to turn off the light. He kissed her on the cheek.

'Sleep well, love.'

Jack stayed for another half an hour, and checked that Mia was asleep. And left, his mother agreeing she'd likely be fine now.

Driving back from Plaistow, he thought about the woman in the baggy tracksuit who Mia had forgotten to tell anyone about. The one who looked like Ellie, but couldn't be Ellie, as Ellie had the perfect alibi because she was with him in the stock cupboard.

Chapter 44

When Jack arrived home, he found Ellie asleep on the sofa. She was seated, her head back, an astronomy magazine on the floor at her feet, which had probably fallen from her lap. Beside her was Jack's Daily Mirror, half the crossword done. The food from their dinner was still out on the table. Not so appetizing in its cold state, the fat congealing. But Jack was famished. He hadn't eaten much of it before he'd had to rush out to his mother's. In a plastic microwave food tray, he gathered some curried beef, mutton dopiaza, various vegetables and rice. He went into the kitchen and put them in the microwave.

While he was waiting, he put the kettle on to make tea. He should keep the surplus food for tomorrow. If he had cling film he'd cover the trays but he didn't. So that was that. And quickly he bundled most of the open trays into the fridge. Tomorrow's supper organised.

Heating done, he settled down at the table to eat, with a large chunk of naan. The concoction hit his taste buds, while his stomach gurgled at the coming feast. He was eating too quickly, shovelling it in as if he were working on bonus. He wasn't going anywhere, there was no foreman watching, so he slowed to enjoy the food, the subtleties of the spices, the texture. It was exactly what the inner man demanded. Or rather, if there was to be no sex on offer, then his number two was an Indian meal.

Or a night out with the telescope? He oscillated on this. Choices. And decided it depended how hungry he was. And what was on view in the heavens.

Ellie moaned and threw out an arm, but was still asleep. He'd rather she was awake, but it did mean he didn't have to talk to her about her sister's morning activity. Mia had seen Cathy with a board by the lake. Presumably to wipe away footprints. There couldn't be any good reason for doing that. Jack had only had a brief glimpse of the body, but recalled the jellied face. It must have been in the water quite a few hours, so Cathy was tidying up after a night time activity. Somewhere too, George was involved. He couldn't think how, the two of them being utterly unsuited, but he was sure the caretaker, one way or another, fitted into the dirty work. Enemies can come together in common cause.

Jack came out of the kitchen with his tea, when Ellie woke.

With a yawn and stretch, she said, 'You were away ages. How's your daughter?'

'OK now,' he said. 'But she's had a trying day. Her mum's in hospital, she found a body in the lake and then her granny took her to an Agatha Christie play stuffed with corpses. No wonder the poor kid had a nightmare. Hopefully, she's fast asleep now, and not dreaming of floating bodies.' He sighed, 'But I'd best keep my phone on in case...'

'Come here,' she said.

'Do you want a cup of tea?'

'No. Just you. With two spoonfuls of sugar and no milk.'

As he crossed the room, a mist of a thought about her sister floated between them. But his body evaporated it like the rising sun.

Chapter 45

Vicky rose from her bed. Her body was heavy and saggy; there was no hope of sleep, although she was thoroughly weary. She'd felt hopeless lying on her back, as if she were about to be sacrificed by events. She must take control. Always she was stronger on her feet, facing oncoming traffic. She shuffled into her slippers and put on her dressing gown, though there was really no need for it. It wasn't cold, no one was around, and it was not as if her nightdress was immodest. She was way beyond that stage of her life.

Already she felt better, standing up.

She left the bedroom, came out onto the landing, and made her way slowly down the stairs. There was no rush. No one was about to admonish her, or had left a mess for her to clean up. She thought, I've been a widow for 24 hours. It was an odd sensation. She would not find him slumped on the sofa, or head on the desk in the home office, his mouth open, or find a puddle of vomit by the toilet. Graham could fill the house, with his noises and smells, his demands. And in a way was still here. Guilt paints strong pictures.

But they will fade, she told herself. They will fade.

In the vestibule, she stopped and looked at the portraits of the various DeNeuves. All the self important headmasters. Well, now a change. They would have to make space for her. A headmistress. The pipe-filled testosterone, the male certainty of the dais – would have to shuffle along, make a space. One or two stalwarts would have to endure the dust of the attic.

And there was Graham DeNeuve, his second best portrait, the other in the school foyer. This one proud in a black gown, perpetually holding a scroll with a blue ribbon tied round. The painter had given him a determined, benign expression. And more hair, and less ruddiness on his cheeks.

'You would not face the world you made, Graham,' she said aloud to the painting. 'Any problems you'd scream at, browbeat and drink away.' She pulled the cord of her gown a little tighter and shifted on the marble floor. 'I could see what was happening five years ago. I told you. And you told me to change the figures and go to the bank...' The blue of his eyes held her; they had that trick of following you wherever you stood in the vestibule. 'Why didn't you die in last year's heart attack? We could have mourned you dutifully. Instead, you came back from hospital like a jubilant Napoleon, back from exile, insistent on your next campaign. With hectoring and drinking filling in for the big guns.' She shook her head and sighed. 'I dread your funeral. The sympathy that will be lavished on me as grieving widow. The rubbish everyone will say about you, how you died in harness, what you gave to the school – when it's we who've been running it the last few years. You were simply in the way, creating needless obstacles. And in the end, what choice did we have if the school was to be saved? Your school.'

She left him, the failed guardian of the flame, and went into the kitchen. That was the portrait she'd most like to remove. But it would be too obvious. She must suffer him a year or so longer. Or there would be comments. What have you done with Graham?

She filled the kettle, switched it on and prepared the tea things. The conversation with Lady Margaret had gone well this afternoon, she reflected. After her commiserations, Lady Margaret had agreed a bridging loan – and would finalise the lease-back after the inquest. The Deneuves would continue running the school as per usual, and pay her back out of future profits. Of course, there had to be future profits. No more messing around with make believe figures. Real profit. They had to bring in more students.

So simple. Why wouldn't Graham see the obvious? Instead, he would have fought all the way to the bankruptcy court.

Fought them too, no doubt.

The police had been sympathetic today. And she let them do their business without obstruction. It would be pointless standing in the way. They would've done their investigations anyway, and perhaps been more searching. She had the feeling it would all come out right. A drunken man stumbled in the lake and drowned. Occam's Razor. The simplest explanation is the most likely.

A few weeks into the school year, the money would all be in then, and she'd be firmly in place before all those shaking heads had time to say I told you so. She must be the Head, so thoroughly that no one would dispute it.

She would be good. She would be remembered. And then hand the baton to her daughters. Which she would not worry about for a while.

She poured the tea into the pot and stirred. And then assembled teapot, cup and saucer, milk jug, and a plate with three shortbread biscuits on a tray. She took them into the sitting room, without a glance at her husband as she crossed the vestibule.

She laid the tray on the coffee table in front of her armchair. The tea needed a few minutes yet to brew. She hated it weak. Tea should taste like tea. Vicky loaded a CD, Tchaikovsky's Pathetique, to break the silence of the house. It was too big for just her. Though Eleanor had said she'd like to move back. She hoped so. Though Eleanor could be messy. Always the compromise when you lived with people.

Vicky settled in her armchair. She yawned, but her head was too active for sleep. It would come. At least she hoped so. These days especially she must be alert.

The caretaker was a nuisance. Be patient, take the blow. For the moment. It had been humiliating writing the letter for him. He had forced that on her, though she wondered whether he actually would have gone to the police as he was already so compromised himself. But his anger had convinced her. He might just be that stupid.

So give him what he wants. Two years of him. Besides, Bramley needs a caretaker. She had never thought much of the deal with the company that gave half price, half competent estate care. She must phone them in the morning and cancel that deal. And hope to get off without a penalty.

Catherine could be so impetuous. She wanted to sort out the caretaker immediately. That wasn't the way to do things. Two years wasn't so long. And George Grove would be bearable. Flatter him. He knew he had to do a competent job or teachers and parents would complain. Just don't rise to his jeers. Let time flow over the stones. The inquest, cremation, done, and his power would weaken by the day. Catherine always hated being thwarted, even as a child. She does create so. Well, Vicky was her line manager now and would teach her the virtue of patience.

She poured out the tea, put in the milk and stirred with a silver apostle spoon.

This house would be too big, whether Eleanor came to live here or not. Not that her daughter would stay long. She'd be off soon enough with her latest whoever. What about the gatehouse? Once the caretaker was gone, she could move in there. That would be fine. Much more fitting to her size. This house could be set up as teachers' flats. Three of them, maybe four, to share the kitchen. It meant she wouldn't have to live with that ancestral gallery in the lobby. She could still retain her garden if she wished, or simply switch to Jenny's. She'd need to do her sums; the rent income from this house might easily pay for another teacher's salary.

She dipped a shortbread in the tea. The idea excited her. There were opportunities. It simply required vision. And patience.

Chapter 46

With only two eggs in the fridge, a couple of slices of bread and a scraping of margarine, Jack was just able to make scrambled egg on toast. Normally he'd have two slices himself, but he had a guest. There was just enough milk for tea. There was the Indian meal leftovers, but hardly breakfast. Tonight's dinner.

As he cooked, he thought of the conversation he and Ellie hadn't had. Her sister cleaning up by the lake. How to start?

He tidied the sitting room table by moving all the crockery and mess from last night's meal into the kitchen. He'd sort it out when he got back from work. Close the door on it, while they ate breakfast.

By the time he had the frugal meal on the table, Ellie had showered. He didn't usually bother to have one himself in the morning. A wash would do. He'd shower after work to wash the day's dust off.

Ellie was chirpy. She'd caught up on sleep and the shower had invigorated her.

'You need a new toothbrush,' she said.

'I'll put it on the list.' He took a sip of tea, then said, 'Were you at your mother's place the night before last?'

She gave him a glare. 'I've told you already, I went home.'

'You didn't tell me.'

'I did.' She sighed heavily. 'And what conspiracy are you constructing now, Jack?'

He ignored her, he'd gone too far to not push on.

'So it was just your mother and Cathy with your father?'

She slammed down her knife and fork. 'Stop it, Jack. First it's George. And now Mummy and Cathy... All involved in drowning Daddy. What sort of warped mind have you got?'

He didn't want to tell her what Mia had seen, feeling guilty enough that his own daughter had somehow got down there to find the body.

He said, 'It's easy enough to drown a drunken man.'

'And you think my mother and sister did that? Or was it the caretaker and his wife? How about his dog too?'

'The police obviously don't think it's that simple...' he began.

'The police are the police,' she shouted. 'That's what they do. They are not some fly by night builder with a pet theory... Don't you ever think? What effect do you think this has on me, implicating my family? On and on, you go. Can you never stop?'

She rose and ran into the bedroom.

Jack was deflated. Though what had he expected? She was right. He was putting her family in the frame without telling her what evidence he had. But if he told her what Mia had said... That wouldn't work either. This was crazy. Ruining the best relationship he'd had in ages. He must shut up. Tell the police of his suspicions, not test them out on Ellie.

He went into the bedroom. She was sitting on the bed, her back to him.

'I'm sorry,' he said.

He put his hands on her shoulders. She shook them off.

'I talk too much,' he said.

She turned about. 'I don't mind you talking, Jack. In fact, I love you talking. But not about this. It's my family. Don't you see? It's where I've spent most of my life. You've been at Bramley just a few days...'

He sat beside her and took her hand.

183

'Your scrambled egg is getting cold,' he said.

'That's more like it,' she said. 'You can talk about my egg.'

'And you have a lovely nose,' he said. 'It fits so beautifully between your eyes.'

She slapped him on the thigh.

'And you have a lovely tongue,' she said, 'and when it's not talking nonsense, it fits so neatly in my ear.'

They embraced. As he held her and kissed, he thought he'd best not apologise again. It would only remind her. Lips still on hers, he began peeling off her t-shirt.

She pushed him away. 'No. Not now. I've too much to do.' She rose and straightened her clothing. 'Come on, let's get in to work. Or people will talk.'

He said, 'What about your scrambled egg?'

'It'll be congealed,' she said.

They went into the sitting room. The egg didn't look that appetizing, but Jack, without sitting down, rapidly finished his. She demurred on hers. So he ate that too. And washed them down with a swig of tea.

'I'll have completed the work this morning,' he said.

'Then how about a picnic at lunchtime?' she said. She clapped her hands. 'We could go onto the island. There's a little shelter on the hill. We could eat – and who knows what might follow?'

She took his hand and dragged him to the door. A last mouthful of tea, and he left the cup on the side as they exited the flat.

Chapter 47

Everything was as Jack had left it the day before. The broken door was lying in the corridor. The smashed piece of doorjamb neatly sawn out to leave an oblong for a new piece to fit in. Ellie was in her classroom just a little way up. They'd left on good terms after their breakfast squabble. In the drive over, he'd taken care to keep off the forbidden. He'd told her about life with Alison, how they met and how the marriage had broken down due to his drinking. These days, sometimes they got on and sometimes quarrelled like children in a playground. He told her about his mother, about what he recalled of their break, too much lost in his addled state. And about making it up yesterday with Mia in tow. It would never be a close relationship. She was too churchy, too judgemental. Maybe he was too. A family trait. But she was his mother.

Ellie had told him more about her continuous feud with her sister. It went way back into earliest childhood. So much of what she'd done at school, she'd done in reaction to Cathy. Playing hockey instead of lacrosse, not having anything to do with science or maths. And often vice versa – Ellie learnt piano, Cathy would have nothing to do with any musical instrument. Or acting, which Ellie did at school and then at University, playing Lady Macbeth in her final year, a part that got her a mention in *The Times* with a comment about her 'devious joy' in her manipulations of her husband. Cathy, instead, took up archery. And got cups for it which she flaunted before Ellie when she came back with her press cuttings.

Nothing, it seemed, was ever done for itself.

Jack thought about his and Ellie's relationship. Was he there because Cathy could never stomach someone like him? A bit of rough to be shoved under her snobby nose. He hoped not, but the pettiness of the twins forced him to see that element must be there. Cathy would never in her worst nightmare consider an affair with a builder, so Ellie must have one, just to slight her.

So what did that reduce their relationship to? Perpetual point scoring. No, he would not believe it of Ellie. She couldn't be so callous, so self serving. They were genuinely attracted to each other. She hadn't come over last night to have a go at Cathy, but because she wanted to be with him. It was not as if Cathy was watching them through CCTV.

Then again, maybe she was. With Ellie as her camera.

Work, the antidote to this circular thinking. Get busy, saw and chisel. He needed to bring the new door and wood from the basement. Get on with it, and stop this *she loves me, she loves me not* rubbish.

Weren't twins supposed to be best mates? Always in each other's company. Dressing the same, phantom pregnancies. He couldn't still his head. That should be a warning. A flare should go up when you can't get someone out of your head.

He set off down the corridor, walking rapidly, passing Ellie's classroom. She was busy typing into her laptop. He would not distract her. Too easily they could end up in the stockroom cupboard – and really, he had to get this job done. He was near penniless.

Love schmuv.

He took the stairs to the basement and switched the light on. The basement had a low ceiling with an assortment of pipes running across. There was a series of interconnected rooms, he had no idea how far it extended, possibly under the whole school. This section was quite full with old desks and tables, cupboards, paint and timber and the doors he was after. There were the computers that George had brought down yesterday, piled on each other, quite a hurried stacking. What went on there, he could to some extent work out. A faked robbery. There had been George openly bringing in the computers to stop the cops finding them. But what did he intend doing with them? He recalled Cathy watching him pile them on his barrow, and George seemingly not giving a hoot. Was it an insurance fraud, with maybe some or all of the DeNeuves in on it?

Oh, what was it to him? Let George make a few quid.

And then he saw the wheelbarrow.

Upside down, immaculately clean as if it had just come out of the factory. It was by the door he'd come down to get – and he knew that the wheelbarrow hadn't been here yesterday when he'd gone down to get a door for Ellie's classroom. So why had someone put it here since?

It was quite a flimsy thing. It wouldn't last a day on a building site. Lightweight, as if for an elderly gardener.

Chapter 48

At the edge of the car park, Jack could see down to the lake where a policeman was taking the tape off the stakes. A second policeman was following him and pulling out the stakes. It was clear they had finished, and would be going soon. He thought of going down to them and telling them his suspicions, but no – they would just be junior officers. The stripes had long gone.

He watched them a while and wondered what they'd found in their searches. Cathy had been cleaning up yesterday morning, but had been interrupted when Mia came. Might Cathy have missed a bit of wheelbarrow track? Not much point looking now, it would be well trampled.

It was a beautiful day, the sun shining in a clear blue sky, sparkling on the vibrating lake surface. Two majestic swans were by the island, while a family of coots swam in a line along the reeds. So peaceful, with the body cleared away, and the cops soon to be gone.

Jack continued to the gatehouse. As he went up the path, he saw the front door was open. It had never been closed since he'd come. Maybe at night. The hallway was less full of boxes and paraphernalia.

'Hello,' he called in.

George came out of a side door and gave him a broad smile.

'Hello, Jack. Nice to see you. Come in for a cuppa.'

He ushered Jack in, and as he passed the sitting room he noted the shelves had been filled. They went through the kitchen.

'Go and sit in the garden. I'll put the kettle on.'

Jack went outside. Instead of sitting down at the patio table, he went to the vegetable patch at the rear of the garden. At the front were two chest high rows of tomatoes, the fruits from green to deep red. Behind a line of bean poles dripping with runner beans. And there at the side was the wheelbarrow, the reason for his visit.

They had a heavy one, a builder's type. Inside were drying out weeds, a hoe and a watering can.

'Hello, Jack.'

He turned about. It was Jenny coming across.

'I'm admiring your vegetables,' he said.

'They're doing so well,' she said. 'Would you like some tomatoes?'

'Love some. Home grown always taste best.'

'Drop in when you're leaving.'

He accompanied her back to the patio.

'Things have changed round here,' he said. 'Correct me if I'm wrong, but you seem to be unpacking.'

'Oh, isn't it wonderful.' She gave a full smile of relief. 'You wouldn't believe how miserable I have been the last few weeks.'

'So what brought it all about?' said Jack.

They sat down at the garden table.

'George went to see Mrs DeNeuve yesterday. On the off chance. And to our amazement, she did an about face. Re-employed us, house back. And I'll tell you what was funny, when George first told me. I wasn't happy at all. I was just thinking of all the work we'd done and all the unpacking we had to do. If anything, I was even more depressed. It was a couple of hours later, it filtered in. It was over. This is ours again. Our home.'

She seemed ten years younger, thought Jack. The stress had gone, plus a good night's sleep. She was actually quite attractive. The last time he'd spoken to her she'd been so gloomy, so non-stop critical of the DeNeuves, that it wearied him listening to her. This morning, she was a different person.

George brought out the tea things on a tray. He set it on the table: three mugs, the teapot, milk and some chocolate biscuits.

'I've got to let the cops out,' he said. 'They're leaving.' And he ran back into the kitchen.

'Getting back to normal at last,' said Jenny.

'I'm very pleased for you,' said Jack. 'I could see how unhappy you were the other day.'

'I was so low, Jack...'

He let her run on, just half listening. He'd seen what he'd come for. The Groves had a wheelbarrow in their garden. They certainly didn't need another, so it was clear who the one in the cellar belonged to.

Jenny poured out the tea.

'George never gets plates,' she said, and was about to go in and get some.

'Forget it, Jenny. I'm not a DeNeuve.'

She laughed.

And they chatted about the house, about getting their jobs back. George joined them a little while later. Jack considered asking him about the computers in the cellar. But thought best not add a sour note to the occasion, but enjoy tea on the patio in the sunshine.

Chapter 49

A staff meeting in just over two weeks, reflected Ellie, when she must have all the curricular work completed. She had discussed it all with the English team at the end of term and through the email list during the holiday. Quite a bit was the same as last year, but some changes in set books, different demands from exam boards. And some scope for personal choice. Cathy was working at the house, so Ellie wouldn't work there, couldn't work there. Unavoidable meetings in the kitchen, flash rows and snide remarks that left her saturated with anger, stuck in what she should have said and hadn't. Not that working here didn't have its problems, with Jack only up the corridor.

But not quite the same problems.

She did like him. If only he wasn't so nosy. This morning, she'd warned him off pretty heavily. Of course, that could have had the reverse effect. *'The lady doth protest too much, methinks'.* Hamlet, Act 3 Scene 2.

She'd better ease up. Try listening, as Cathy might say. Bitch. Or maybe just nod sweetly. Not always so easy.

At least the police had gone. She'd heard them talking in the car park. Then the cars had driven away. And she'd popped out to look – and had seen that they'd gone from the lake. No longer a crime scene. No more of them crawling about in those white plastic overall things, looking for heaven knows what. And hopefully not finding anything much.

To work. She was so easily distracted. She hadn't used to be this way. At university, she could work through the night shutting the world out. It was her sister, being so close to her these days. Cathy always did this to her.

Go away.

Macbeth or *Romeo and Juliet* for Year 8? She preferred *Macbeth*. A good man gone wrong. She could sympathise. The Scottish play then. *Pride and Prejudice* or *Great Expectations*? She'd done *Pride and Prejudice* for four years in a row. Heaven save her from the Bennets. She'd give Pip a run out and release herself from three terms of drudgery.

She was busy typing when Jack came in the classroom, pushing a wheelbarrow.

She stared at him in surprise.

'Why have you brought me my mother's wheelbarrow?'

'I found it in the cellar,' he said.

She scratched her head. 'I don't understand.'

'It wasn't there yesterday morning when I was last down there.'

She was wary now, wondering what was coming.

'Meaning?' she said.

He sat on the front desk, a few feet from her.

'You went home the other night,' he began, 'leaving your sister and mother at home with your very drunk dad...'

'Don't start again, Jack,' she said quietly.

'Hear me out,' he said, holding up a hand. 'The two of them dragged him out the house and ferried him along the path in this wheelbarrow...'

'How do you know?'

'I've never seen a wheelbarrow so clean, except in a shop,' he said. 'And why's it suddenly in the cellar?'

'Why?'

'Because they were afraid the cops might see it.'

'It doesn't follow, Jack.'

'So you tell me why it was in the cellar?'

She could think of no reason to offer him. It was there for the reason Jack had guessed. To keep it from the eyes of the cops. And she couldn't come up with an alternative.

'Keen gardeners use their wheelbarrows in their gardens,' said Jack.

'Go on with your scenario,' she said, her neck itchy. She shifted uncomfortably, knowing she must keep her temper.

'Where was I?' said Jack. 'Right. From the house they wheelbarrowed him down the path. Then put him in Cathy's car and drove down to the lake...'

'How do you know he went in her car?'

'Because we saw her in the car park scrubbing the car out as if she'd driven through a sewage farm. Your father was a stinky mess. I know, I wheeled him to your place. And Cathy wanted every particle of him washed away.'

'She often washes her car at school,' said Ellie feebly.

'Coincidence on coincidence,' said Jack. 'Sometimes there's just too many. Let me go on. When they got to the lake, they put him back in the wheelbarrow, pushed him to the edge and tipped him in. The perfect crime, until George turned up. Walking the dog, I suspect. Couldn't sleep, stressed out about moving and losing his job...'

'How can you know George was there?'

'I've been worrying about those computers,' he said. 'I keep seeing them. First we saw them in the boathouse, and yesterday, he brought them into the school. Out there in plain sight of Cathy, he's carting them in. And he doesn't give a damn that she's watching. I watched her, angry as hell but doing absolutely nothing. Why's that?'

'You have all the answers, Jack. Tell me.'

She was breathing heavily, squeezing her nails into her palms in an attempt to still herself.

'Because he had something on her. Something a lot bigger than stealing computers. Murder. That got him the house back, his and Jenny's jobs. And he thumbed his nose at her when she saw him bringing the computers in.'

'Blackmail,' she said.

'He gets what he wants and all Cathy can do is yell, as he witnessed her and your mother down by the lake...'

'My God,' she exclaimed. A real cry, at his closeness. 'You can't be right on this. It's not possible. There has to be another explanation.'

'When I first told George about Mia finding the body, I sensed he was lying to me. That he already knew,' said Jack. 'And then bingo, he gets his house and job back. Luck? Or what?' He paused, keenly watching her. 'So how else do you read it?'

She was silent for a few seconds, thinking quickly. This was no time for the big protest.

'Mummy and Cathy have been acting oddly the last day or two,' she conceded. 'I've felt excluded from conversations. I came into the kitchen yesterday and they shut up. Like they had a secret.'

'One hell of a secret.'

She bit her lip. 'What are you going to do?'

'Go to the police.'

'Oh hell,' she cried. 'I don't care about Cathy. Let her rot in Holloway or wherever. But my mother... This is awful.'

'This is murder.'

She got up, striding about the room. It needed no acting. He knew so much. What on earth could she do?

'When are you going to the police?' she said.

'You're not going to tip your mother and sister off?' he said, suddenly alerted.

'Of course not,' she said. 'They deserve what they get. But I want to come with you. Back up your story. Is our picnic on the island still on?'

'Do you feel like a picnic, with all this hanging over?'

'We could talk it through while we are eating. It's as private as you can get out there. Make sure it all hangs together, then go to the police.'

'Makes sense,' he said. He slapped his head. 'How am I going to get paid?'

'Give me your invoice. I'll take it over to the house. Tell Mummy you've finished, and I've OK'd it. She keeps petty cash there. I'll bring the money over with the picnic.'

'Thanks, Ellie. That's a relief. I so need that cash.' He got up. 'I'd best get a move on and finish the job.' He pecked her on the cheek. 'See you lunchtime.'

She grasped him and pulled him into an embrace. They held tight, clutching, finding succour in lips and softness for their very different reasons. They broke and searched each other, uncertain which way to go.

'I must finish up,' said Jack, torn.

'You must,' she said. 'I'll sort your money out.'

Quickly, he left her.

PART FOUR:
PICNIC ON THE ISLAND

Chapter 50

The door was hung. A little stiff at first. He oiled the three hinges and it swung sweetly. Just enough gap off the ground. A simple enough job, but always satisfying.

He wasn't impressed by the door lock. A feeble thing. But then again, you could just break the corridor glass into the computer room. Might have been better if George had done that. But it was all a game anyway. Making the money go round and round. Smashing doors and windows and repairing them again. He hoped Ellie could get him his payment. He had only a small job to follow this, and had to get Mia back to Brighton. And eat, pay bills. Live.

Just the lock to go in. He marked up where it would fit in the door, and where the plate should go on the doorjamb. Don't rush this bit. He'd learnt that often enough. Get the marking up right. Or you spend twice as long doing an inferior job.

Square and tape. Get it right first time.

He'd just completed the drilling for the lock when his phone rang. Annoyed at the interruption to his flow. He looked. This one he'd better answer. And keep calm. Especially if she'd been talking to Mia.

'Hello, Alison,' he said warily.

'Hello, Jack. What have I been hearing about Mia and dead bodies?'

Straight in, no messing. She had been talking to Mia.

'Only one dead body.'

'That's one more than enough,' she said. 'What on earth was she doing wandering around on her own?'

'It's a school,' he said, attempting a defence. 'Perfectly safe. Normally.'

'So you did a risk assessment, did you?'

'It's a school,' he insisted. 'I didn't think there'd be a body here. Be reasonable.'

'I am,' she said. 'As reasonable as any concerned parent can be. I concede, you didn't know there was a dead body in the grounds. I'll put that down to bad luck. Though I sometimes wonder. But you did let her go down to a lake on her own. Isn't that so, Jack?'

'I didn't know that she'd go down to the lake. I was busy working.'

'She said you were busy with a woman.'

That shut him up completely. Mia had dropped him in it. Not that he didn't deserve it.

'I don't know what to say about that,' he said. 'I left her in the library with videos and books... And I got talking to a teacher. And er... well...'

'Spare me the details, Jack. I'm not interested in your sex life. Only where it concerns Mia.'

With some relief, he said, 'She's with my mother now.'

'I know where she is. She phoned me ten minutes ago. And I'm happy she's there. But tomorrow I want her here. Midday. Can you manage that?'

'I can. How was your stay in hospital?'

'Fine. I'll see you tomorrow. Midday. And please don't let her wander about on her own. She's only eleven, Jack.'

She rang off. Leaving him a pendulum swinging between fury and guilt. She was right, she was wrong. He still had no idea why she'd gone into hospital. To catch him out? He wouldn't put it past her.

He was a lousy father. One sniff of sex and he lost all responsibility. She was right. Sod her. Mia should not have been wandering about on her own. There was a lake. Not very likely she would've drowned in it. She can swim. Maybe even less likely there would've been a body in it.

Bad luck. And, okay, some irresponsibility. Happy now, Alison?

But at least it was out in the open. Alison knew. And she'd calm down by the time they met tomorrow. He had to be in Brighton by noon. That money had better come or he was going nowhere.

What a life!

About time he had some stuff on Alison. She could be careless enough when she had a boyfriend on the go. Hoity-toity now, all queenly and self-righteous... But then again, she was in hospital with some unknown ailment.

Enough of this. He was sounding like Ellie going on about her sister. He was in the wrong. Leave it there. Don't blame Alison for bawling him out.

But how could he not?

Back to the lock. He could be reliably sure it wouldn't scream at him. Lecture him about risk assessment. Or give him orders about when and where to drop his daughter off.

Chapter 51

The lock was in the door. He was working on the last bit, the socket and plate on the doorjamb. Finish it and he could be away. A picnic on the island – and who knows what that could lead to? There were trees and shrubs there, nicely obscured. A secret place. Odd, considering it was a prelude to a visit to the cop shop. Reflecting, he doubted there'd be any sex on offer. Once the case was laid out, and Ellie could see all the implications for her sister and mother, he doubted she'd be in any mood to take her clothes off.

Might it not be better to go straight to the police station? Except he'd promised her. She was getting all the food prepared, maybe at this very moment. He could hardly suggest that they go to the police, get her mum and sister safely arrested and then have their picnic.

But was doing it this way any better?

He was chiselling out the remnants of wood in the socket, having drilled out as much as possible. A pity there wasn't a square drill bit to drill square holes. In fact, he thought, it wouldn't matter what shape the bit was – the hole would still come out circular when it was spun in the chuck. He often had daft thoughts.

That's what working on your own did to you.

His head was all over the shop, like a classroom of screaming kids, the sensible ones at the back the least heard. He'd hate anyone to read the muddle of his mind. Sex, money, telling the police how to do their job, Alison, returning over and over to sex, lunch – he was hungry. That was the loudest kid, the one rubbing his stomach. All he'd had today was the toast at breakfast and a couple of chocolate biscuits at the Groves'.

And here was the bringer of food, coming down the hallway. In one hand a large basket with a big handle like Little Red Riding Hood, in the other what looked like a tablecloth. An orange scarf was tied in her hair, gypsy fashion. She was the goddess of the picnic. How could he ever think he wasn't going?

'Will you be much longer, Jack?' she said when she got to him.

'Ten minutes,' he said. 'What's in there?' indicating the basket.

'A few things. Ham, eggs, olives, cream cheese, tomatoes and spring onions from Mummy's garden, bread, grapes, plums and fizzy water...' She stopped a second. 'Something I've missed...' She clicked her fingers. 'French butter.'

'My stomach is churning at the sight of it.' A sudden thought. 'You didn't say anything to them?'

She shook her head. 'I simply went into the kitchen and prepared this lot.'

'Weren't they curious who it was all for?'

'I told them it was with you.' She laughed. 'There we are, it's an official picnic. Like being engaged.'

'Walking out as they used to say.' He grinned.

'You're my boyfriend now. Aren't you?'

'I am.' He was almost tongue-tied. The picnic was a seal. The bride price. Or something or other. He was welling with love. Such a beautiful thing to do: row over to the island, eat the feast, make love... forget the dirty work to be done afterwards. But it couldn't be forgotten. He just hoped it wouldn't ruin the party.

If only he'd said nothing. Too late. He couldn't have avoided it. He had to tell her. No matter what.

She said, 'Oh yes, and this.'

She took a fat, unsealed envelope out of the basket and handed it to him. He flicked through. It was full of twenties.

'Oh, you're wonderful,' he said.

'I am, aren't I.' She did a girlish twirl. 'You said ten minutes, Jack. Well, if I stay chatting you'll never finish. I'll wait for you at the boathouse. But make it ten minutes. Not a second longer.'

She kissed him on the cheek. He wanted to hold her and get a little more, but she'd already pivoted about and was walking away. She half turned to him and waved a strict finger.

'Ten minutes.'

Chapter 52

Ellie was in a rowing boat at the landing stage of the boathouse as he came down the hill. The job was completed. He'd swept up, collected his tools together, but would go back to put them in the van after their picnic. But now he was free, no self-reproach about wasting time. And he'd been paid too.

A police station to visit. Save that. Worry about it post lunch. Though it would have to be talked through. He'd have to be careful on that topic.

She was on the middle thwart, her back to the prow, oars dangling in the rowlocks. The basket was at the end of the boat, the cloth laid over the seat. Ellie was obviously going to row, making Jack feel as if he was in the middle of a fairy tale. He was the chosen one, the poor woodcutter, whom the princess was going to row out to her enchanted island.

What would he find there?

She tapped her watch imperiously. 'What time do you call this? Fourteen minutes. I nearly went without you.'

'I didn't realise this was a regular service.'

'We have a timetable. This is the island ferry.' She bowed and indicated the back seat. 'You are in first class, sir.'

He climbed into the boat which wobbled as he took his seat. He felt he should be rowing. That's what men did for their girlfriends.

'I could row,' he said.

'I am sure you can, Jack. But not as well as me. I've been rowing on this lake since I was six. I rowed for Uni. I'm a Blue, you know. You'll be perfectly safe. Can you swim?'

'A bit. Though I'm hoping I won't have to.'

'You won't,' she said and pushed off the stage with an oar. And began rowing.

She did it effortlessly. Smooth strokes, no splashing, obviously enjoying herself.

'I haven't done this for a couple of years,' she said. 'It's amazing how my body knows exactly what to do. All those early mornings on the Isis.'

He couldn't keep his eyes off her, her movement like a dance, the swans and coots her underlings. She was in complete control, delighting in her body's rhythm. The glinting surface like a sprinkling of musical notes.

'It's wonderful here,' he said.

'Surprising what you get used to. Most days I just don't see it at all,' she said without breaking her stroke. 'It's why it's lovely to see it through your eyes.'

'I can't imagine owning a lake,' he said.

'I can't imagine not.'

She stopped an instant and looked behind her. There was a landing stage in the reeds of the island. He could almost hear her calculating angles and strokes.

She began rowing again. One side, then the other, then both and the boat eased into the island's landing stage. She brought in the oars.

She said, 'Do we have to go to the police, Jack?'

Suddenly alerted, he thought: she has been talking to her sister and mother.

'We don't have to,' he said, without conviction.

'Meaning we do.'

He was silent, and all at once afraid. He was in her domain. Across the water, in her rowing boat, about to alight on her island.

'Meaning I'm not sure,' he said. Which he knew was no good. Unsure today could go to the cops tomorrow.

'I'm sure it's the right thing,' she said.

'Are you?'

'Of course.' She looked him hard in the eye. 'It's murder. Daddy deserves justice. We all do.' She waved her arms. 'But let's have our picnic before we go over the details... You carry the things up to the shelter. I'll tie up the boat.'

He stepped onto the stage and bent down to pick up the blanket and basket. She'd crawled to the prow and was holding a rope.

'Can you see the shelter?' She pointed it out, it was just visible at the top. 'We used to call it the castle. Somewhat flattering. I'll follow you up in a minute.'

Jack set off with the basket and cloth. There was a crude path up the hill, beside it bramble, nettles and various yellow and pink flowers in clusters. There was the shelter up ahead. He could see it clearly now, a weathered wooden thing, like a country bus shelter, at the crown of the hill. There would be quite a view from there.

A great place for a picnic.

He looked behind him for Ellie. And was puzzled. She was in the boat, on the rowing thwart, the oars back in the rowlocks. She pushed away from the shore.

'Sorry, Jack!' she called. 'I really am.'

It was then he turned back to the shelter. And out of it came Cathy in shorts and a yellow t-shirt. She was holding a loaded crossbow pointed at him.

Instantly flooded with fear, he threw the basket at her, dropped the tablecloth and ran. Ellie had delivered him up, an ultra performance, with picnic and tablecloth.

He scuttled through a patch of nettles and behind a tree. His arms were itching from the nettles, the least of his troubles. Pressing into the tree, he listened and couldn't hear her.

Thwack!

A crossbow bolt struck the trunk. He peered out from the side of the tree. How quickly could she reload? She was coming through the nettles, face utterly concentrated, reloading. And a new bolt was in. So few seconds.

He'd hoped he might be able to get to her before she could reload. But he'd have to be so close beforehand that she could hardly miss.

Jack backed off down the slope. He was off the path, not knowing what was possible on this part of the island. He backed behind another tree, somewhat thin, and pulled himself in.

Thwack!

How many bolts did she have? It wasn't like a six gun where you could count. She might easily have a dozen. Twelve attempts. And she'd won cups, her sister had played Lady Macbeth. What a talented family! A thought struck him: how had she got to the island? A boat perhaps on the other side. If he could get there... And then he rejected it as the truth slapped him. Ellie had rowed her over, and then come back to collect her target.

Where was Cathy? He couldn't see or hear her. He listened. She was hunting him, listening for him as he listened for her. Predator and prey. She knew this island backwards, whereas he had no idea where he was going. Just away.

Thwack! A crossbow bolt struck him in the calf. He was in trouble now, stumbling, leaning against another tree, torn by brambles across the arms. Why in the calf? He was thinking rapidly. To slow him, to add to his misery. She didn't want a sudden kill. Not for her sister's lover.

He'd be shot through like a pin cushion by the time she'd done with him.

His boot was squelching from the blood that ran into it. He was surprised he could still run on it. Though it ached like hell.

If he could make it to the reeds, perhaps there'd be a chance. Hide in them. But on the island itself, he was simply her quarry.

Thwack!

A bolt into his other calf. She was playing with him. Slowing him up for the kill.

He thought of surrendering. Walking out, hands up. A mad idea. Cathy hadn't come to take him prisoner but to silence him. That's why Ellie had lured him here. He would be buried somewhere on the grounds. His tools with him. His van abandoned miles away. How long before he was reported missing? Alison would probably do so in a few days. The DeNeuves would say they'd paid him for his work and that was all they knew.

Why should anyone think otherwise?

A wave of nausea rocked him. He was shivering and sweating, legs trembling, liquid in both boots, arms scratched on thorns and briar. He eased down the slope, moaning from aching limbs. Where was she now? He had a fear she might have gone round him. Could be waiting the way he was going. She'd jump out from behind a tree. A final shot to his head.

He was light-headed, paddling at the water's edge. There were ducks homing in as he threw out bread, his mother with him singing *All things bright and beautiful, All creatures great and small, the Lord God* – no, no that wasn't right. He couldn't remember the line. Something something, *the Lord God made them all*. It desperately mattered, he had to remember the line. His mother would shout at him, smack him.

All things wise and wonderful.

That was it! *The Lord God made them all.*

With the ducks all around him, gobbling bread, water paddling at his feet, he sang:

The rich man in his castle,
The poor man at his gate,
He made them, high or lowly,
And ordered their estate.

A swan was coming for him, head forward, beak pointing. It was Cathy. He was on the island, he recalled. She was trying to kill him. There she was, behind that tree, up the slope. The landscape flitted in and out of focus. He slid down, crawled through undergrowth, briar and nettles on his isle of dreams. His mother was somewhere. He didn't want to go that way. There were the reeds. Moses would be floating in a basket. He would see the pyramids beyond as in the picture in his junior bible. Except there was the landing stage just a few yards to his left. He remembered, he was on the island. He must escape from the Egyptians.

There was Miriam, in a rowing boat. She was pulling in. She didn't want to leave the basket in the bulrushes.

'Quick! Quick, Jack. Come on!'

Yes, he was Jack. Where was he?

'I should never have agreed,' she cried. 'Quick, Jack! Please.'

She wasn't Miriam, she was Ellie. In a boat at the oars, beckoning. She'd come to save him from the Egyptians who had spears and crossbows. He pushed through the reeds to the landing stage. Stumbled onto the platform, fell to his knees, and Ellie dragged him into the boat. He fell down flat across her knees.

His feet were liquid, his head full of bees. The land of Milk and Honey. The picnic. Cathy had been trying to kill him. There were arrows in his bleeding calves. Why weren't they rowing away? Leaving Cathy across the Red Sea. He could hear gurgling. The mud sucking in the reeds. He looked up at Ellie, and couldn't quite work out what he was seeing. Blood was pouring out of her neck like a bubbling fountain. He turned his head and saw a crossbow bolt through her throat, feathers sticking out one side, the point the other.

He must row. Could he? He wasn't in Egypt. He must get away from the island. He took an oar, stupidly pulling it out of the rowlock. The crumpled body of Ellie was in his way. He rose. There was Cathy on the landing stage, the crossbow fixed on him.

He staggered, twisted and swung the oar with all his remaining energy. It smacked hard at the same time as a bolt slammed into his shoulder, forcing him backwards over Ellie, and down onto the decking. Winded, he lay there.

The Philistines are coming!

He lay there for centuries. Where were the Philistines? Were they fighting Caesar's army? He pushed on Ellie's knees to lift himself. She was a ragged heap, her neck all blood, soaking into her t-shirt, trickling down her arms.

The oar was still in his hands, the blade end broken off.

Jack looked over the side of the boat. By the side of the landing stage lay Cathy, face down in the water, blood seeping from her head, the blade end floating nearby. Her arms were splayed out as if she were trying to swim away. The crossbow lay on the boards of the landing stage like a discarded toy.

He thought of getting it, but the effort, and to what end? Instead, he took out his phone. It was soaked in blood and it would not work. Of course. The Ancient Egyptians did not have phones. He must row up the Nile to Memphis. Find Potiphar.

His head was pulsating, the world vibrating. This was not Egypt. He was not Moses or Jacob. He was Jack. He was bleeding to death. He saw Ellie's phone in her belt. He pulled it out. It was blood spattered but alive. He dialled 999. And waited.

Was this modern times yet?

Tears welled when a female voice answered, 'What service do you require?'

'Ambulance and police,' he said. 'I'm bleeding to death.'

'Ambulance first then, sir.'

He was put through and explained where he was, not in Egypt but at Bramley, and that he'd been shot with a crossbow. When he said it wasn't an accident, they asked more questions. He could not cope.

'Please! please!' he cried. 'Just get here.'

They said they'd come with the police.

He lay the phone on the thwart. Ellie was splayed out on her back, mouth wide open, blood dribbling from it down her cheek. He could barely move, aching and weak. There was a bolt through each thigh. Symmetry, he thought. Quite right for Cathy, the mathematician. Pythagoras's theorem, congruent triangles. A piece of bone was poking out of the fabric of his shirt.

He wasn't carrying any bones. He'd come for a picnic with Ellie.

A face loomed up at him. It was George in a rowing boat.

'What a dog's dinner!'

'Ellie's dead,' Jack said feebly. 'The crocodiles are eating Cathy. Can you row me to Memphis?'

'Sure, mate. Lay on your side. Can you do that?'

'I think so.'

He wriggled until he was stretched out on his side, his head cushioned on Ellie's thigh.

'I'm going to tow you back,' said George. 'You'll be alright, mate. Leave it to me.'

At which point, Jack gave up. Neither in Egypt nor Bramley. And just dimly aware of a rope being attached. Less aware of the movement of the boat across the water. Completely deaf to the sirens and to the efficient paramedics who stretchered him to the ambulance. And set off, siren blaring and at full speed, to the hospital.

Chapter 53

Vicky came down from the house. She'd heard the sirens and the vehicles arriving, and knew there was trouble. She'd been out in the garden weeding her vegetable garden. She'd gathered radishes, spring onions and beetroot to have later. Her hands were still dirty. She should've washed them. It wouldn't have taken a minute.

She got down to the boathouse as Jack was being taken away on a stretcher.

'Is he alive, Mr Grove?' she asked George.

'Just about.'

Quickly, Jack was loaded in the ambulance. And it shot away, the sirens crying out its urgent mission. Out of the school gates, the wail dying away over the next minute.

She sighed. 'Just about' wasn't good enough. It had to be all or nothing. She should have washed her hands.

And then she saw Eleanor splayed out at the bottom of the rowing boat, her flesh blue-white. She was going to call for someone to do something, when the puddle of blood and the bolt through her daughter's neck checked her.

Vicky wept, leaning against the boathouse sobbing uncontrollably. Her beautiful Eleanor gone forever.

Recovering for a moment, she looked up to see George rowing two policemen out to the island. She feared to ask anyone why they were going there, dreading the answer. But watched compulsively. It was difficult to see clearly what they were doing out there, beyond pulling something into the boat.

And so she waited with the others, like a fisherman's wife awaiting at the quayside for news from the lifeboat crew, as

George rowed back to the shore. It would be Catherine they had picked up. Was she alive or dead? It had all gone wrong, so quickly. Eleanor had been so full of life barely an hour ago. She'd told them that Jack knew everything and was going to the police after their picnic. It seemed a simple idea to dispose of him on the island. Out there, and Catherine so proficient with a crossbow. She'd won cups and prizes.

It had almost worked. Jack was pretty far gone. Just about alive. And then something had gone awry.

Eleanor had been shot.

On purpose or by accident? Considering her daughters, it could be either. Her beautiful Eleanor. So talented, so full of promise.

And Catherine? Might there be hope for one, oh please God, one of them.

The rowing boat pulled into the landing stage by the boathouse. George stepped out and tied up. And the two policemen dragged and carried Catherine onto the stage. Vicky sank to her knees; they gave her space.

'My poor girl.'

She stroked her daughter's head, she could feel a crack in the skull. Her flesh was as pallid as a chicken hanging from a hook, blood congealed in her hair. Her mouth had an ooze of froth between the lips.

Both gone.

She shivered. It was all so pointless. Her family evaporated. What good was Bramley without them? What good was she on her own?

A policewoman came over to offer commiserations, but she held her off.

'Please, leave me be. I'm going home.'

And she stumbled back to the house. She couldn't stand all the people, gawping at her daughters. At her misery. Seeing her sin out there in the plain air.

An hour later, a detective sergeant came up to interview her. Water was seeping out the front door. There was no answer to his ring, so George took him round the back, through the garden and into the house that way.

The water was running down the stairs in a steady stream, coursing over the marble floor. They followed the stream back up the stairs to the first floor bathroom. There was no answer to their call, so they broke down the door. And found Vicky in the bath, her wrists slashed with a barber's razor.

Chapter 54

George sat awkwardly on the plastic chair. He held a bunch of flowers and some grapes but didn't know what to do with them.

'Leave them on the side there,' said Jack pointing out the space. 'I'll get the nurse to put the flowers in water and wash the grapes when she comes round.'

George did as he was told, grateful to be rid of his burden.

'How are you, mate?'

'Not too bad, considering,' he said. 'A broken shoulder bone, two calf bones pretty cracked up. I lost a lot of blood but once they had me in here, I was not in any real danger.'

'You heard about Mrs DeNeuve?'

'I read it in the paper. She killed herself.'

'Me and the policeman broke down the door of the bathroom,' said George. 'She was under water, the bath filled to the brim, taps running full, water pouring over the side, and her wrists slashed. Razor on the side, empty bottles of pills lying about, she was making sure alright. Too late to do anything. Drowned, poisoned, bled to death. Take your pick.'

'Whole family gone,' said Jack. 'First her husband...'

'Then Catherine, we fetched her over from the island. The bitchy one.'

'She was the one out to kill me.'

'Killed her sister,' said George.

'That was an accident,' said Jack.

'You sure?'

'She was shooting at me,' said Jack. 'Ellie got in the way.'

'Not everyone thinks that,' said George. 'Not that it matters in the way of things. Catherine killed her whether she meant to or not. And we can't ask her.'

The images were too clear to Jack. Ellie sprawled out in the boat with a bolt through her neck, her sister coming at him with a crossbow. That was the vision he'd woken to several times in the night.

'The school's finished,' said George. 'Down the drain. The receivers are in. A dead headmaster they would have got over. But his missus too? She was going to be the new head. And on top of it, the head of maths and science going berserk with a crossbow, killing her sister, head of English. The place has gone bung. The phone's ringing non-stop. No one to answer it. It's a waste of time me doing it. What can I say? I've got no authority.'

'So what's happening to you and Jenny?'

'Not as bad as you might think. Receivers don't act that quickly. And we saw a solicitor and he said hang on in there. They have to give reasonable notice, especially with a family. And if they don't, then we take 'em to court. The court will be sympathetic. Give us six months, maybe more.' He slapped his thigh. 'I was worried sick when I heard the receiver was coming. Well, he comes. And I take him over the school, tell him about what's happened and everything. Put him in the picture, take him back to our place, give him a cup of tea. He's quite a nice bloke. He says the school needs security, and as I'm on the spot – will I do it? No point saying no to that, was there? All considering.'

'Glad you're not out on your ear, George. At least you've some time and a bit of cash coming in.'

'That's the way I see it, mate. Could've been a lot worse.'

They were silent a little while. Jack was achy and shifted in the bed. It was hard to get comfortable with his shoulder, and his legs in plaster. They'd given him sleeping pills last night. But he wasn't the only one uncomfortable. George was rubbing his hands together as if they were cold.

Jack said, 'You might have been able to save Cathy.'

'I thought she was dead,' said George, looking down at his feet.

'You could've dragged her onto the landing stage.'

'I thought she was dead.'

'You left her to drown.' He paused, then added, 'The second person you've done that to.'

'What do you mean?' His head jerked up.

'I mean Mr DeNeuve. You saw the three of them drowning him and you saw your chance to do a deal.'

'How can you possibly know that?'

'Ellie told me.' It was a lie, but he chanced it.

'She's dead.'

'And so conveniently is her sister.'

George was sucking his lips, struggling which way to go. He raised his hands as if to surrender.

'OK, I'll tell you. I was out walking the dog. And I saw 'em all down by the lake. And I thought why should I rescue the bastard. So I did a deal.' He stopped, and stared at Jack. It was all out. 'You going to tell anyone?'

'No. I don't see the point. And I doubt if they could prove it with the family all dead.'

'I appreciate that, Jack. Thanks, mate.'

He wasn't sure he wanted thanks. If George wasn't a murderer, he was the nearest thing to it.

'What's happened to my tools and van?' he said.

'They're all safe. I collected up the tools. They're in the house. Get 'em and the van whenever you want.'

'I'm here another couple of weeks. At least. And I won't be driving for a while. My van's safe for a while at the school?'

'No problem. You mend. I'll keep your stuff safe.' He leaned in closer. 'I was wondering whether you might need a bit of cash...'

'I got paid for the job,' said Jack, 'but that won't last long.'

George said, 'I could give you a loan, no rush to pay it back. I've come into some money...'

'Let me guess. From the sale of computers?'

George shrugged. 'What's the point giving it to the receiver?'

Jack thought about it. It was tit for tat. George was thanking him for keeping quiet. Not that he was going to the law anyway. Should he take it? The DeNeuves were well and truly dead. The receiver didn't need it. Just some anonymous creditors who could claim off the insurance company.

'The loan would be useful, George. Be a couple of months before I can work again. So, yeh, to tide me over. Thanks.'

George looked at his watch. Jack doubted he was in a hurry to get anywhere else, but he'd come to do what he had to. And he knew himself that hospital visits always get to the boredom stage, when words run out.

'I'll come and see you next week,' said George.

'I might be walking by then.'

Chapter 55

After George left him, Jack was low. He didn't like taking George's money, but couldn't afford pride. Or too much morality. Things were going to be rough the next few months.

At least he was alive. That hadn't seemed a likely outcome when he was running about the island with Cathy taking pot shots. George was suggesting that she'd killed Ellie on purpose. That hadn't occurred to him. But then he'd got a lot wrong when it came to Ellie.

She'd come back for him. Dragged him into the boat. If she hadn't done so, then most likely he'd be dead and she'd be alive. That last moment, the instant when both he and Ellie had been alive, when Cathy was coming in for the kill. But to kill whom? Seeing her sister trying to rescue him...

Did she shoot Ellie to stop the two of them getting away?

Or had it been an accident? Well, hardly an accident, but she was aiming for him, and Ellie got in the way.

As she always did.

It hardly mattered, as George said. Cathy had killed her and Cathy was dead. Who she'd been aiming for would never be known. But her father's murder was clear enough and her attempted murder of Jack was proved beyond doubt by the crossbow bolts they'd pulled out of his legs and shoulder. Two counts would take her down.

If she were still alive.

Why did he care? Ellie was dead. Her betrayal hurt as much as the crossbow bolts. So happy, so free and open as she rowed out on the lake – all the time leading him to Cathy. But then she'd come back for him. At what point, as she was rowing back, did she turn about and think, I can't let my sister do it?

She'd come back for him.

He knew too much, and not quite enough. He hadn't allowed that she was in on her father's murder. Didn't want to allow it. There was the maddening truth of it.

Ellie, oh Ellie.

He hated the woman that had rowed him to the island. He loved the woman who'd come for him.

A little later, Mia and Alison came. Alison wore a summery yellow dress and was bearing flowers, Mia had a bag of cherries. He was oh so pleased to see them.

Alison picked up the flowers lying on the side. 'Look at these! Whoever left them there?'

'George, the caretaker, came,' he said.

'Men!' She blew out her cheeks. 'Does he think nurses have the time to put flowers in vases and wash grapes?' She picked up the grapes too. 'I'll get some vases and wash the fruit. Give me the cherries, Mia.'

Mia handed them over and Alison left them. Mia sat down.

'We came the other day, Dad, and we had to go away as you were having an operation.'

'Yes, they put a pin in my leg. To hold the bones together.'

'Why do you get into all this trouble?'

Mia always gave him the tough questions. Not that he could deny it was a fair one.

'Because I'm stupid,' he said.

'I read in the paper that a woman tried to kill you,' said Mia. 'Was it the woman I saw you kissing?'

'No,' he said. 'She tried to stop it.'

Not strictly accurate, or, rather, true at one point if not at another.

'It was all very complicated,' said Mia. 'I saw it on the news and read it in the paper. Three women in one family dead, and one man badly injured. You.'

'Famous at last.'

'I don't want you famous for being dead, Dad.'

'Oh, thank you so much, Mia.'

'Would you like me to read you something?'

'As long as it's not gruesome.'

Mia took a big, fat book out of her backpack. 'It's the book I borrowed from that school library. Do you think I should take it back?'

'Keep it,' he said. 'You had a hard time there too.'

'I don't want to ever go back to that place,' she said.

'Nor me.' Though he knew there'd be a last visit, a month or so hence, to pick up his tools and van. To make his living again.

When Alison returned, with two vases full of flowers and the washed cherries and grapes in a bowl, Mia was reading to Jack *Harry Potter and the Half Blood Prince*.

Thank you!

I am grateful to every reader who finishes one of my novels. I have taken you on a journey which I hope you have enjoyed. There are plenty of things you could have been doing, other than reading this book. So, thank you for your time.

If you liked **Jack o'Lantern**, here's what you can do next:

I'd appreciate a review on Amazon. In that way, you can help me tell other readers about my books. Without reviews authors get few sales on Amazon. So I'd be grateful for your review to help this series get on the move.

You can get a **FREE** ebook of **Jack of Spades** if you sign up for my readers' list. You may give it to a friend if you wish. Every month a lucky reader from the list will be sent a **free**, signed paperback of their choice from the series. Sign up using this link:

http://eepurl.com/buAh5H

When you sign up for my readers' list you will receive my regular newsletter. This will give you news about me, what I'm reading, tell you about my future books, PLUS a variety of giveaways.

Books by DH Smith

DH Smith is the name I use for my Jack of All Trades series. The books are all standalone novels and can be read in any order.

Out Now:
- Jack of All Trades
- Jack of Spades
- Jack o'Lantern
- Jack by the Hedge
- Jack in the Box
- Jack on the Tower
- Jack Recalled

Coming Soon:
- Jack At Death's Door
- Jack At The Gate

Books by Derek Smith

All my books, other than the Jack of All Trades series, are written under the name Derek Smith.

Mystery/Crime
Murder at Any Price

Fantasy
Hell's Chimney
The Prince's Shadow
Elektra

Other
Strikers of Hanbury Street (short stories)
Catching Up (poetry)

Young Adult Novels
Hard Cash
Half a Bike
Fast Food
Frances Fairweather Demon Striker!

Children's Novels
The Good Wolf
Feather Brains
Baker's Boy

For Younger Children
The Magical World of Lucy-Anne
Lucy-Anne's Changing Ways
Jack's Bus

About the Author

I live in Forest Gate in the East End of London. In my working life, I have been a plastics chemist, a gardener and a stage manager before becoming a professional writer. I began with plays, working with several theatre companies, and had a few plays on radio and TV, as well as on the stage. In the early 80s I became involved in running a co-operative bookshop and vegetarian café in Stratford, learning to cook, and having my first go at writing a novel. The first was a mess, and, after too many rewrites, binned. The transition from drama to novels took me a couple of years to get to grips with. My first success was a young adult novel, Hard Cash, published by Faber. Buoyed up by this, I stuck with children's work, did school visits, and made a hand to mouth living as a full time author, topped up with some evening class work in creative writing at City University and the Mary Ward Centre in Holborn. A few adult fiction titles appeared from time to time, between the children's list, and I have since been working more in that direction with my Jack of All Trades series.

My full name is Derek Howard Smith. I write as DH Smith for my Jack of All Trades series; all other books appear under Derek Smith. Earlham Books is my own imprint.

www.dereksmithwriter.com

The book you're holding was designed by Lia at Free Your Words...

Contact lia@freeyourwords.com for a quote

www.ingramcontent.com/pod-product-compliance
Lightning Source LLC
Chambersburg PA
CBHW060210180626
46813CB00007B/2769